ONE

The White Room

Y. K. Sozer

Table of Contents

Klara 4

One 9

Mr. Gregorev 20

Two 27

Mrs. Simi 38

Three 45

Maritime Hotel, New York 53

Four 61

Mr. Oliver 68

Five 75

Mr. Aziz 86

Six 94

Hilda Kenwood and Jacques Arlo 104

Seven 111

Sister Abigail 118

Eight 127

Mrs. Sullivan 138

Nine 149

The Dreyfus Family 157

Ten 171

The Club House, Manhattan 184

Eleven 192

Chloe 203

Twelve 215

Klara 221

Klara was amazed at herself when she realized that at that very point she was wondering how handsome this guy was at the same time as she was trying to scribble down the mailing instructions. Usually she wouldn't easily bring herself to care about the looks of a guy she dated, so why was she doing this now? In the middle of a very important conversation with the very important Mr. Gregorev? Obviously, it was only his voice that was very attractive anyway. So, what would it matter to her if he was good-looking?

"One," said Gregorev. "I would like you to write about 'One.'"

"Like the number?" asked Klara.

"One," Gregorev said simply. "Whatever 'One' means to you."

"Since I will not have a chance later on, perhaps I could ask for a little help? When, who, where? Can you give me anything, any clue?"

"If you are describing antiquity, don't list the weapons and mines," said the enigmatic Mr. Gregorev. "Or if you are talking about a poet, don't let this be his biography. Etc., etc. Take a journey into your mind, and let your soul accompany you. Then reflect so that I can read about your travelling tips. Amaze me, Klara. Do something different, something that's not been seen before. You have three weeks. Don't be late."

Klara realized that she had not properly said goodbye only after she hung up the phone. With an open mouth, she remained motionless. Did the very great Mr. Gregorev just ask her to amaze him? This by itself was enough of an excuse to let the laughter finally escape from her lips.

She started to make her own living by working at odd jobs and not so odd ones afterwards. Despite the fatigue, monotony, corporate wars, and discontent that always seemed to appear no matter where she worked, Klara continued to write. For her, writing was part of her daily routine until it evolved into an inescapable indulgence. After a while, she decided to look for someone who would take her writing seriously. As is the fashion, she would go on a date, giving in to too much pressure from people around her. But her true passion was to write. She would live her parents' life one day and until then there was still time. Now, she was pursuing another kind of personal ambition.

When she coincidentally met and befriended Mrs. Simi, and despite her rich imagination, she had never anticipated that life would carry her to where she is standing today. She was shivering with joy, excitement, and the need for haste as she started to prepare herself for this three-week journey of a lifetime. She had never liked pressure; but she knew how to be in command of it. She would not let pressure take over and she would prevail. Nights would be long, and days would be unbearable.

So, Klara got to work and started to read. Finding her old notes and gathering her favorite books, she sat at her computer. To begin, she would choose a town to write about. But there would be no mention of a restaurant in her memoir of this holy town, the home of three monotheist religions. She made a road map where religions would follow to merge in "oneness." Sipping from spicy teas and occasionally wine, she read, reasoned, and imagined what she would come to write in these next few weeks of adventure. By the time she started to write, she no longer cared whether Mr. Gregorev would like it or not. She wrote what she wanted to write.

Not a word more.

Not a word less.

It was complete.

It was whole.

It was "One."

One 〜

Thou shalt have no other gods before me.

Thou shalt not make unto thee any graven image

Thou shalt not take the name of the Lord thy God in vain.

Exodus 20:3-7

I'm calling on Archangel Ariel quietly. I need to be encouraged. They say, "Don't ask many times when you need something from the angels. Just ask once, and then let it flow. And the answer shall come." So, I lose courage again; did I ask too many times?

Whatever "one" is telling me is what I am writing now. Am I doing this right? Should I continue? I long for a sign now, just a little sign. And I shall follow. I am looking for that sign on the ground, in the air above the clouds. Then, I hear that song on the radio.

"Calling the Angels" is what is playing.

"I need a sign to let me know you are here. And I won't give up if you don't give up."

The White Room

I am happy. This is not a place one can get to so easily. You need to earn it. Or, you must realize that you have earned it.

Anyone who can do that can go into that room. However, this may happen only after purifying their heart.

This is by far the best journey that a soul can take.

Everything and everywhere is white here. Not a cold white, but a soft white. Although I cannot tell the pistachio green, peach pink, and sweet pale blue, I know they are there.

This is a waiting room. I retire in this room from time to time. When I hit rock bottom, for example. Or right after I beat myself up when I know I could have done things differently. Or only when I forgive myself for a past transgression.

This is a place between dream and reality.

This is an ethereal place: where none can touch, no words can harm. I can only watch there.

This is a static place: where there no air, pressure, or humidity exists. Not a person, no materials, no form, no matter subsists. No voice, no words. Not even imagination, only eternity.

There, only I exist.

There is nothing but unending serenity in this void. As the void envelops, so does serenity. I can sense the scent of orchards although I cannot smell. Even if everything here is white, an apricot-colored smile riddles my face. Funny how I cannot see but I know. Or maybe I am secretly hoping that I truly have an apricot-colored smile. With these serene moments, I am cheating on life: one cannot escape there and still make a claim on life. What I am trying to say is that one cannot be a part of life with that state of mind, one can only watch. So, then I put on another smile, this time a playful smile.

Not only is it not possible to be a part of life from this dimension, it is not necessary, either. I am enjoying it for now. I will return eventually. For now, I am hanging on to it as a guilty pleasure, and it is mine so far as I let it be. Perhaps it's a few minutes but it's worth an eternity. One can hang on to that moment and stay still in nothingness. Just stay still. But to live, one needs to leave. Come to think of it, there is no chance to even wiggle since there is no air. A person eventually has to leave. And at that moment, I remember the story of that little girl. Is this really a good time? I sacrifice the last good moments of my pleasure and start thinking about the story while I have a glimpse of eternity.

When she was a little girl, she enjoyed the path she took to school very much. She would take the chance to be late and stop by every leaf, every beetle and observe them slowly and carefully. She would catch a rainbow on the drop of dew on a leaf; and could tell every beat of the hymns the beetles sang. She could smell the scent of freshly baked buns and bread in a bakery, miles away; and enjoy their taste with no need to eat. Her palms were so sensitive that she could know feelings without touching, and she could heal others with her touch. But she was not aware that she was different; she thought everyone was like this, and that everyone could hear the voice of silence.

She could be at two places at the same time. She knew, actually she could sense that other experiences like this were possible. But this was a little complicated. She wasn't sure if other people were familiar with this phenomenon. She knew that a guy from her class also had the same "thing."

One day when she stayed in the classroom during recess to finish up some homework for the next class, there was the quiet guy with freckles who stayed behind as well. He was sitting two desks away and facing her. The windows were open, and the nice weather was breezing in.

The boy with the freckles turned to her and said, "I can watch you from the ceiling up there. Did you know?"

"No," she answered. "I do see you right in front of me, but I did not know that you could watch me from the ceiling."

"I can levitate and look down from the ceiling although I am sitting right in front of you. Look! I'm right there above that bulletin board on that wall," he pointed out.

"I believe you can do that," said the little girl. The bell rang.

They never talked about this again. After a while, the boy moved to another town and they never saw each other again. They were not meant to meet again: The boy was there for one reason and one reason only—to make her aware of the depth of time in space that is subject to variation. She was already moving through time at a fixed speed and direction; but had no frame of reference for it.

She called them "day dreams," and she would always come back to the place and time she started from. Now, she knew more.

That Same Year

"Is there really a God?" she asked her grandfather.

Grandpa did not know exactly how to reply. This is what he ended up saying:

"The very fact that we can question the existence of something shows that there is existence. Even the answer 'no, there is not' shows that 'there is.' Because in order 'not to be,' first it needs to 'to be.'"

She tried to understand. Grandpa, seeing the struggle, asked her to bring a glass of water, and drank the whole thing at once.

"There is no water," he explained. "I drank it and finished it. But there had to be water first before there was none. If there were no water, I couldn't have possibly drunk it. We cannot talk about the nonexistence of something that does not exist in the first place.

We pulled out the dianthus in the backyard, remember? If they weren't there, we couldn't have possibly pulled them out.

Maybe we could have pulled out others but not the dianthus. And now let's try something more intangible. Love perhaps… We would need to ignore everyone who loved, who was touched by it, who handed it to the next generation, who suffered from it in order to declare that 'love does not exist'… Maybe we cannot hold it in our hands; but bearing witness to the way it is expressed with words, taken shape with actions, and the consequences it arouses are a good reason to defend its existence."

Grandpa then went silent. "Did I go too far?" he thought.

The little girl, on the other hand, had understood. And she never questioned it again.

And the grandfather wondered if the day would come when he would tell her more. If it did, he would surely say:

"If you think there is more to be said about this question, you are absolutely right. This question has been asked since the beginning of time. Civilizations went down and rose again because of this question alone.

Too many wars, philosophical assaults, political games, and racial maneuvers were carried out because of faith or its endgame."

"Is there God?" he asked himself.

"Endlessness," he thought. Having neither an end nor a beginning.

To be all: to exist in all.

To mean the end of everything when you talk about the end of anything.

To end all.

He is "One."

And He is "All."

He who exists in all.

Whose existence is indisputable.

Because the existence of one is the existence of all.

We are all but one in endlessness; We are Him; we return to Him.

You cannot separate a grain of sand or a servant of his apart from Him, for this segregation would be but an insult to His oneness.

Endlessness: you cannot end that which is endless, thus there is no endlessness.

Existence: how could you disprove the existence of existing?

He exists in everything that exists.

He has no shape, time or place: He is everything.

How can the existence of "everything" be questioned?

And He, who is in everything, is "One."

And God is Existence.

And He is the "One" in everything.

Grandfather went on to water the garden. Despite what he had said about the dianthus, they were very much alive. And they were there waiting to be watered.

The little girl had her answer. She believed then and there and never again questioned God and His "Oneness." She would learn to use this for a greater good in time. But, it was not the time yet.

In those early years, when she was fully aware of the many facets of life, on that sweet spring day when the summer breeze was in the air, she sneaked from the house to the nearby shore. She dove into the pleasant waves as if she was moving from this world to another. She felt as if she was a small island in the middle of the ocean and there were no others. She heard not a sigh, not a sound. But the whole of creation was with her; she could feel every single being within herself. The little girl giggled as if being tickled by the water moving along her body. She did not know what this was, but it felt like she was coming out of a daydream in the middle of the day.

My time is up in the White Room. I need to descend now and start to fight, if need be. It was intended for the White Room only that I remained in solitude. And as I come down, I know there will at least one more person next to me. Then maybe a few more, and many more. And perhaps one day one of them will come up to me and let me know that even though I must fight, I am allowed to sit and wait for the chaos to pass over me. I can hear this now. And perhaps also will add: "Even if you are stressed—and you will be stressed—don't be scared. Whatever the outcome may be, don't hurt yourself or be sad; just go on and do not be scared."

Deep down inside, this is what I want to hear. You know what? I'm already scared. What I know is that I am not afraid of the charges upon me; I know how to fight those off; but what about the chaos that I, myself, create?

Soon, when I return to my life, I will take command of some of the wars, and a few may even be fought because of me. Some will fade away, but others will be bloody. And most probably it will be me who will shed the most blood. Until I learn otherwise.

"Do not give up" is what the angels told me.

I will not give up.

Until the circle is round.

And I am "one."

I will not give up, until I return to "One."

***

Klara put a little note at the bottom saying she was in Jerusalem and then mailed the package.

The anxious wait of one week could now officially begin.

Mr. Gregorev ～

It was almost sundown. This was his favorite time of the day. He poured a little Dalmore and lit the cigar he'd been holding onto for some time now, enjoying the New York skyline before his eyes. Patel's collection this year was pleasantly surprising. He could spare a few moments to think about the interesting phone conversation he had earlier.

"I want to give this girl a chance," the voice on the opposite end had said. "There's something I cannot name in her writing. Well, of course I can tell, but I want to be sure. Please do keep this in mind when you approach her. Go after her, shake her a bit. Let her unveil. But, do not scare her. I don't want her to run away. All I want to know is how deep she can dive."

"Understood. I will uncover her depths through my methods," he responded.

"Jan," Mrs. Simi continued. "I am, of course, aware of your reputation. As I am sure Klara is as well. Your methods precede your reputation; it is all well known. So, I want to emphasize that our goal is to get to know her deeply and not scare her away. Yes, there is an answer to the question that is bothering you now. You are wondering why I am taking the high road to get to know her by involving you in the picture, when we have plenty of candidates around to write."

'This old lady is really a witch', he thought. 'But a sweet one. I don't know if there's any instance where she cannot read others' thoughts. I don't think so. Sometimes I truly believe she has a disguised electronic scanner to do the job'. Then, he got angry at himself. What if she also read the 'sweet witch' bit? Partially to amuse her and more importantly to end this conversation, he responded, "Yes, I am curious about my involvement, and what else you can tell me about this intriguing new candidate."

Being among the powerful playmakers in town and a mysterious one at that, Mrs. Simi said that she was following her intuition, based on feelings inspired by her own life story.

The publishing house they worked at was only one part of a philanthropic giant that also housed charities, think tanks, and leading institutions in arts and sciences. Mrs. Simi was actively involved in these other organizations as well. As far as the publishing company was concerned, she simply oversaw everyone and everything, yet made it look it was done effortlessly. The staff knew about her deep commitment and appreciated her efforts despite her age, which must clearly be more than a few junior staffers' put together!

call people by their first names. The monument of authority that she was, Jan Gregorev always believed that Mrs. Simi took life too seriously with all those charities and things she was trying to exert her influence over all the time.

The crackling sound from the fireplace brought him back to the present. He leaned over the pages he had received from Klara as he took another sip. He hadn't been anticipating anything like that.

"Aha," he'd say after finishing a quick first-read. He wasn't expecting this; she actually managed to amaze him. "Let's see if she can keep it up!" The next round would of course be "two." Would she be able to capture the essence of "two," he wondered? One was whole and complete. But with two, things would start to change. "The other" would come into the picture, and peace and quiet would start fading away. Two was another beginning since all other numbers would follow only after "two." Would she be able to pull this off?

He wanted to send Klara a message; mystical yet simple, distant yet encouraging. It was too early for a face-to-face. He had to come up with something else.

Klara,

Holding this note in your hands means that I found what you wrote promising. How precious is it to understand, appreciate, and relish that "oneness" in Jerusalem? Not without a cost, but surely priceless. I'm confident that you enjoyed the ride too, as I see you find yourself being one with that little island in the middle of the ocean in the end. I'm reading you correctly, right? You must like the ocean. Or, at least I hope so.

I'd like you to leave your white room now. Yes, your second subject is "two."

Clear your mind, sharpen your pencil. Watch Beauty and the Beast perhaps; but let the tales deal with naiveté. I will be waiting for your next essay in three weeks.

***

Klara became insanely happy to find the envelope in the post box she rented. She read the note in a single breath. Small island and all, how could he possibly know? She felt naked and embarrassed. Then she thought about their mutual passion for the ocean and took note of the clue suggested by his reference to Beauty and The Beast. But her silent cry came with the last sentence.

"Please call me Jan."

Was this just an innocent game for Mr. Gregorev—Jan—or was he truly interested how deep her pen would go? Clearly this wouldn't be a first for Klara to get to the bottom of the meaning of "two."

Their paths had crossed before, two's and Klara's, that is…

Klara knew well about it: She encountered it, lived through it, been petrified of it. Then she learned to stand up to it and transform it.

She could well write about it to Jan.

"Two" was duality.

Two ∼

"Love your neighbor as yourself."

[28] One of the teachers of the law came and heard them debating. Noticing that Jesus had given them a good answer, he asked him, 'Of all the commandments, which is the most important?'

[29] 'The most important one,' answered Jesus, 'is this: "Hear, O Israel: the Lord our God, the Lord is one.[a] [30] Love the Lord your God with all your heart and with all your soul and with all your mind and with all your strength."[b] [31] The second is this: "Love your neighbor as yourself."[c] There is no commandment greater than these.'

Mark 12:28-31

I'm calling on Archangel Raziel, the keeper of secrets, quietly. To guide me in this puzzle that has only two steps so far. Secrets always had an important part in my life. It wasn't a life full of secrets, but it was surely adorned with them. Although I have never been interested in people's secrets, I've always wondered what secrets made people do. As for the secrets of the

Today, I am trying to curb the devil in me; the angel is doing just fine.

But tomorrow, I know I will question this: Should I be dominating the devil in me?

And if I do so, will the angel still be there? They are a duo, aren't they?

The devil is there to be the devil. If he is done, what will the angel do?

Why are we making such a fuss over the devil then?

And why should we spend so much effort and time to try to understand, forgive, love those who we do not love; do not get along, who we are angry with, who we are cross with?

Why should we tolerate the bad inside our neighbors when we cannot even make peace with the one in ourselves? How does "two" dare to do this?

We need to understand the "two;" "the duality" in search of "the totality."

Two, perhaps due to its nature, has two phases.

The visible side says, "There's good and there's bad." Understand this. You know what to do with "good." Think about what you will do with "bad." Know when to get close and when to stay apart. Be in command. Because "bad" will not just appear, for example, at an exhibition. You could perhaps encounter it on a mountain top and not at the exhibition about that mountain. And if it is at the exhibition that you encounter each other, be thankful. Because this is a very generous lapse before you face the real one.

This is how it all happened…

We were two people that day, a duo trying to decipher the secret of two.

Two is a tough number. Luckily, we knew each other well and we had each other's back.

It did make her restless that we were a duo. She does not like two. She surely trusts us both, but not "two," which is capable of playing a double game. I, on the other, had no fear. I was content that she was with me.

We were headed to this exhibition in the city that we both very much meant to see. Following a lot of mishaps from clogged roads to sold-out tickets, she told me that "we weren't meant to see this exhibition." The exhibition was inspired by a volcano in Italy. And volcano meant destruction.

"We shall not be a part of that destruction now," she said. "Nor shall we share it."

"So, is the volcano always destruction? Will we not be able to go near it or to an exhibition of it?" I remember asking.

And she answered, "Not necessarily. It is today that we understand this here and now and let it go. Think of it this way; the good is not inevitably always good and bad is always bad. Or today's good and bad may not be the same as tomorrow's. Just that.

On another day and at another time we can safely visit the volcano or the exhibition. Our lesson today is to understand and show that this is what is meant for today. And this is important how? We can control the duality in us and in everything else as we start to grasp it as such. Simple, yet effective."

Just as I made peace with the fact that "we shall not become a part of the destruction that day," and headed for the exit, a man approached as if he had specifically chosen me among everyone there and offered two tickets. "I want to sell these tickets," he said, then adding, "Heck, I'll even give them to you for free."

I remember telling him, "We cannot accept them; but thank you. We shall not be a part of this, not today."

The concealed side of two, though, whispers this: "It is not enough to understand it. You need to execute as well. You need to be in peace with both of those souls in universe. That 'duo' is there to give number 'two' it's due. And, there is no third next to good and evil."

Good and bad.

Better and worse.

Be ready for both.

It was brought to light later on how I underestimated my supposed understanding of "duality." Not on top of the volcano but in the middle of the ocean. And it was a little too late. Not fatal, but definitely very late. We were at this little precious town by the ocean on a beautiful weekend. The unfortunate events to follow began with a traffic jam, again.

Traffic gets stuck always and everywhere. But the officers in charge somehow seemed unusual to me. They were right in front of me, donning their flashy vests with an 'x'—do not enter—marked on them. They forced us to make a 'u' turn, to go back. And yet we still drove forward. Why were we still driving? Did I not understand?

Finally, we came to an intersection. We should either take the service road or go on the highway and head back. We took the service road. To my surprise the name of this road was the same as the one we lived on back home. We drove for a while. And no matter how far we drove, the road dragged on. Ultimately, as we reached the shore, I noticed a café with the same name as one near our house. All the signs seemed to point us toward home. But, we did not heed them.

In that beautiful weather, and in the middle of a joyful vacation, I did not suspect that any "bad" would come and find us. I understood duality, but I did not really know it. There may be "bad" hidden in "good," and it may show itself to you occasionally. And most probably, it does this not because it wants your friendship. This may well be a warning to you: do not turn a blind eye.

At this point we started to sail. A horrible storm throttled us in the middle of nowhere. It pounded us long and good with steady rain and tireless winds. The storm quieted eventually, but not my guilt.

The fish did not whisper, but I thought I heard them so…

"There was a man fearful of greed and jealousy. But he was both greedy and jealous. He would at times dive in these waters and pray that the waters would wash away what he could not unburden from himself alone. He would walk away a different person at the end. The waters would gather up his greed and jealousy inside an orb and occasionally fire it up in what you would know as a storm."

It was one of those adversities that day.

Had I understood that and had we have driven away, none of these events would have happened. Now that this was the case, I too asked the fish:

"Am I not supposed to fancy his greed and jealousy? Is this not the bargain? If we are to do this thing right— the act of being a good human—we need to accept each other in every way, and then bear the consequences. So why am I feeling guilty now? Because I am not happy about his greed and jealousy! Especially since it was poured down upon us both…"

And the fish answered:

"You could not stop what happened to you; you did not see the signs. Even if you had noticed them, you failed to perceive their significance. You were too nonchalant, too immature. You shouldn't have turned a blind eye.

So, what should you have done? Just like in any situation of chaos, you should have resisted being a part of that storm, that destruction. You needed to accept the making of a man with the good, bad, greed, and jealousy that comes with him; but you are not to be a part of its outcome. That was your lesson."

I understood. But I did not say anything to the fish.

We were two people trying to uncover the secrets of "two." She had solved mysteries before me, I knew even if she did not say so. Those who are used to unchaining doors recognize their kind when they meet.

I wanted to talk to her about my share of the deal until I was breathless. To talk about this endless combat between the good and bad; as if she hasn't lived it. To show how much I tried. That I did not comprehend this wholly before, but that I know better now. That I have been deceived by adamancy, that I was deluded by wickedness and then had to end up humoring the "bad." I wanted to talk about all these things over and over again. I needed her to pat my back and tell me, "All is well." I needed that affirmation that it was "not my fault," and I needed her to console me. Finally, I wanted her to know that I understood that bad is part of good, but I still needed time to master it. I wanted to tell her these things because she is straightforward. That is why

I am a little anxious. Because if I am wrong, she will not hesitate to say it to my face—that I know.

And she told me:

"When you counteract with good and bad enough times, and as you relive those experiences that are not so innocent, you finally learn to accept the greed and jealousy of those you face. And that's when you forgive yourself. Yes, forgive. And you watch your intoxicated triumph melt in the humble fires of the universe. Because it is then that you are ready for some other quests, other adversaries, and other conquests. Now, leave these behind for there are other questions out there. Go after *them*."

So, I was relieved.

As I comprehend that I can command those wars I attract upon me, I also realize that I can end those wars just as easily as I start them.

This is only the beginning, I know. Neither will chaos stop here, nor will I learn easily. I also know this.

I place the invisible face of "two" in my palm and I make peace with it.

And on one of those nights when all prayers are answered no matter how busy the angels are, I pray knowing that they will hear me and everyone else regardless.

I know this is not something I will do always. I do not and will not call you out lightheartedly. I am not revolting, nor pleading.

But tonight, I am calling on the Devil in my friends and foes alike.

"If I cannot heal you;

I will fall back.

If I am not the one to make you feel better;

I will fall back.

Can you hear me?

Hear me out and go.

In every darkness; there is light.

Go and find your light;

Go find your angel to heal you.

But, if you still want to be the Devil, contain yourself and be the Devil with an angel sleeping on your shoulders.

That's when I will love my neighbor."

Mrs. Simi ～

What a blessing it was that fate was on her side! First Jan and now Klara. No doubt she was interested in both for more than what they each possessed; one being a communication guru and the other a skillful writer. And now there were other issues and other people that needed to be focused on. She would not make future plans on assumptions anyway. Things needed to mature. She was hopeful; actually, she needed to be hopeful.

Mr. Gregorev had joined this little game, despite his reservations. It was not that important what he thought at this point. Suffice that he was playing along for now. They were really at a very early stage and this adventure did not have the luxury to end poorly. Mrs. Simi was not hiding its importance, at least not from herself. Klara must have sent another nice piece since Gregorev was talking about "the next subject" that day. Klara was not just a pretty face, and this was promising.

It was a good start, worthy of a celebration. Her darjeeling tea was a good choice for this occasion. She followed the mist taking over her tea cup and indulged in thoughts of her early travels to London in her youth.

She could almost savor those tea sandwiches again in her mouth which reminded her how hungry she was. She could have a light bite just about now.

Mrs. Simi was a petite, middle-aged woman with her butterfly framed glasses constantly hanging on her neck. She was always a treat to talk to. Nobody knew her areas of responsibility in the publishing house, let alone her story, because she was the most senior of all. Yet everyone liked and respected this kind tea aficionada. It would go without saying that she was a good manager. When things start to go south, she would appear from nowhere and point out the ways and means to solve the problems. She would do this so inconspicuously that people would almost believe that they just gathered around the solution and brushed off the crisis themselves.

Mrs. Simi would receive invitations to many events in the city thanks to her position and connections. This became especially handy when she started to keep tabs on Jan. After following him for a while, she eventually came to understand that he was exactly who she needed. When she was ready to introduce herself, they finally met at that panel organized by the Defense Department.

She gazed at the priceless view of the park. Everything was changing so rapidly. Towns, people, and traditions were almost shedding identities from one phase to get ready for the future. It was impossible to stop this change, and perhaps unnecessary. Yet, there was one task to follow: to safeguard the knowledge and pass it unharmed to the generations to follow. Now, *that* was important. And equally important was to find the beacon holder before the jubilee.

The cucumber and smoked salmon sandwiches that Mr. Oliver brought satisfied her craving perfectly. As she was savoring these delicacies, she was proud of herself for the choices she made with these two, among that list of ten people. She still needed two more candidates. The remaining six would not be easy to eliminate. Yet she knew that these two she chose would be the ones to lead. It would just require a little more patience...

How proud would the grandfather be? Not hers, Jan's, of course. She personally had met the elders of the Gregorev family, many years ago, in Europe. Mr. Gregorev surely didn't need to know this. She'd met Klara's as well, but that was more complicated.

The next day, as she was streaming through the reflections she carried along from the night before, she paused when she found herself thinking about Jan's grandfather. "He would enjoy a good cigar just like his grandson," she thought. And as she wondered what drove her to thinking this, she saw Mr. Gregorev standing at the doorway of her office. "How curious-what we perceive with our five senses revives the memories that we thought we had long forgotten? For instance, the scent of the cigar you've carried along reminded me of a journey I made to the South of France many years ago."

"Maybe this is a sign that it is time to visit Europe, Mrs. Simi," Gregorev said. "What do you say? A nice vacation in the Old World? You are working tirelessly more than ever."

"Mr. Gregorev, this proposition sounds lovely. But who will take on all the work if we go on such a journey?" she asked.

"Oh, no, Mrs. Simi. I could not possibly accompany you, no matter how much I may wish to. Among many other projects, I'm heavily invested in a project with Klara's essays as well. But as I said, a nice vacation would be good for you and I can definitely handle what you leave behind."

"Mr. Gregorev, I will think about this and I don't think I need to tell you that there shall be no funny business in my absence." Mrs. Simi had no intention to go anywhere. But she wanted to remind Mr. Gregorev that her eyes were always watching him. And Gregorev made a quick and relaxed hand gesture, meaning "I would never" and left rather joyfully. Mrs. Simi was smiling playfully behind the young man as she thought, "the simple dervish is no stranger to the hipster in him in these prime years."

The young man started to plan a nice first encounter after he gave his assistant the note he wrote to send to

Klara. The plan was to make it a little mysterious and a little flirtatious.

Klara,

When I look at the deep analogies you used in "two" and "duality," I hope you do not think that I was trying to sway you by pushing the "Beauty and the Beast." I was hoping to give a simple starting point to reflect and not at all undermine the potential you have already shown.

At least, this was my intention. And I say this, because this is how I approached it when I was first given the "talking points" and was inspired by the Commandments. My sleepless nights and full days would end up with similar paragraphs. And just maybe because of that, I wanted to be next to you when you were caught up in that storm. Because I also was a victim of similar storms and spoke with those fish as well. Trust me… I love the ocean, too, I told you this. And I also know what it means to walk through the storm.

I am not playing games with you, Klara; I respect the angel and the devil inside you. They both *make you write all this. One does not exist without the other. I know "two" well.*

Those signs that you learned to interpret are no strangers to me. I do have signs I trust and follow. And those I know too well; hence I remain cautious. But, the angels? They are new to me… Perhaps I know them as well, but I don't know what I know?

Who was that next to you when you got to know "two"? Don't tell me. I hope she is there for "three" and "four." For me, it happened to be so. As for "five," I have other plans. We shall wait and see if fate has already painted that scene and is waiting for us to put the plan in action.

Klara, in three weeks, do not mail out your notes. Go to that café under the Maritime Hotel. I am sure you can get a nice, decent table this time of the year. Your notes will be personally retrieved."

Was this all a joke? Klara was pacing in her apartment trying to make sense of the note she just received. Was Gregorev aware of what he wrote? Did he understand the meaning of his words? At the very least, he must have read what she wrote attentively. This was good news.

She wrote about monotheism in "one" and, although she could do otherwise, in "two" she took the path referencing the commandments. She chose to follow the signs, and the guy noticed this? The guy: meaning Gregorev? Gregorev: meaning Jan? "Oh God," she thought.

Not only that, but he was also talking about himself following a similar path. Was this a coincidence or was the guy having his way? Was he sincere about the things he was writing or was this just a game for him? But why would the mighty Mr. Gregorev play games with her? His words: "awaiting the plans drawn by fate," what was *that*? Was he trying to make moves or really making an effort to connect philosophically? "Of course, the latter," she said to herself, "and you should feel ashamed to think otherwise! Get a grip on yourself."

Nevertheless, she knew this: They somehow have taken the same path and reflected on it by writing similar things. At least Jan was saying so. Perhaps, this was a tryout. If Jan was sincere – and when one thinks with a more rational attitude, it would appear he was – he had ended up with similar conclusions in his own essays. "He must have understood and appreciated her," she thought, and this alone was a great achievement.

Now she was filled with enthusiasm and joy. She had an idea about the next essay, "three," but she had to work on it. Equally important was what she was going to wear in three weeks. She blushed when she realized what she was thinking. Perhaps this would be a tête-à-tête? She once again fell into despair after catching herself for what she was visualizing.

Three ~

8 "Remember the Sabbath day by keeping it holy.

9 Six days you shall labor and do all your work,

10 but the seventh day is a Sabbath to the LORD your God. On it you shall not do any work, neither you, nor your son or daughter, nor your male or female servant, nor your animals, nor any foreigner residing in your towns.

Exodus 20:8-11

I hesitate a little before I call out. Do angels take a vacation? Maybe take the weekend off? Friday, Saturday, Sunday? Or, do they need to work for six days and take the seventh off perhaps? I know the answer a little, but I ask the question anyway. Because there is plenty of time. Because it is Saturday today. And I also want to know this: What is the rule for those who need to work ceaselessly or for those who need to be there for things to "go on?" My answer is not ready; I will think a little bit more. No need to rush, it is Saturday after all. And considering all this, on this beautiful

Saturday, I call on Archangel Raguel, quietly. Dear Archangel Raguel, please shower us with peace and serenity. We need it deeply to find our answers today.

1, 2, 3, Go!

…Sensation…

1, 2, 3, Hush!

…Silence…

1, being the one and only, will be the first and remain first.

And 2, because it is following 1, will always be the second and never the first. Yet will pave the way for 3 and 4.

But more importantly, 3, will be the first where we pause.

There is no hesitation in 1.

And you do not want to take a break in 2.

But 3?

Either to take a little rest or gather your breath to move on, there is always a "fermata" in 3.

Just as in birth, life and death.

Today is Saturday.

End of the week.

The day of the Roman God Saturn.

The Roman calendar year would end and be celebrated with Saturnalia. According to the legend, the slaves would trade roles with their masters; eat, drink, enjoy, and savor the taste of freedom just like them. In so much so that, if a slave was to laugh and talk too freely, he'd be asked if he thought Saturnalia came too early and would be punished.

The celebration perhaps dedicated to the prosperity of land is also attributed to Saturn, the God of sowing. It is also about fallowing the land when it is the time; about fertility and fruitfulness.

Saturnalia is such a time that "time" is frozen, roles are exchanged, land is fallow. For those who do not let go, who cannot let go, it is a time when the word *Saturnalia* is softly whispered. In short, it is a time to take a break, a time for *fermata*.

Today is Saturday.

Today, we have time.

And today, we are "three."

There are two of us, and then there is the little girl: a little girl from a dream.

Three.

We will pause, we will contemplate, and we will dream a little.

Perhaps, we will go about to look for that lost word we meant to find for so long.

The lost word is a name.

The name of the little girl.

The name of the little girl in the dream.

Long ago, she dreamt of the little girl, and she loved her. But even in the dream, she wouldn't let the reigns loose. She was too old to bear a baby, so, she only saw her from behind. The little girl had beautiful, long hair. So beautiful that she couldn't bear to look at the little girl.

"I can't bear to have her," she said. "Not at this age."

They graciously touched her shoulder.

"Most beautiful," she said.

"Yes," they answered. "And very smart."

She smiled vaguely and started to wait for her.

She knew the girl would not come; we knew. We were looking for a name nonetheless. As we were feverishly chasing it, the name would mockingly play hide and seek with us. As we got more driven, the name would hide further from us. This is why we were playing this game; we were hoping to find something else as we were following the name. What we were hoping to find, not knowing what it would be, was our "third." This, we knew. We did not know our third, but we certainly loved her.

Three is completion, because for the first time, there is a dimension.

It is "standing up," becoming a triangle from a line.

The body was always there. Mind as well, and it progressed so much to reach some invaluable heights. But soul, it was there perhaps even before the body: it always was there, and it always stayed there.

We may not know in what sequence they were bound together. But to stand up, all three elements had to be there. Body, mind, and soul finally and only found the third dimension when they were stuck together, and then they rose.

This is important how?

Man, who now stands up, would first run to Saturnalia and then beyond to reach today.

But first: The Book of Daniel

As we were running after the "lost name," we came across a story about "learning to pause" in the Book of Daniel.

Daniel, when interpreting a dream that the King of Babylon, Nabuchadnezzar, had recited that the King would lose his power, might, and mind for 7 years and only would come back to himself after accepting the rules of heaven. Also, the legend would so have it that Daniel also wrote his book after 70 years of exile.

Despite the abnormalities in the Book of Daniel, which seemed to be a collection of works comprised of words from several languages that was the work of different people and times, it contained a prophecy not to be ignored about a future leader to come:

²⁴Seventy weeks are decreed for your people and your holy city: to finish the transgression, to put an end to sin, and to atone for iniquity, to bring in everlasting righteousness, to seal both vision and prophet, and to anoint a most holy place. — *Daniel 9:24-27*

And the prophecy wouldn't stop there. It would be seven weeks before the new prince comes; then the new city would be rebuilt again in 62 weeks, but the prince would then be killed. And the seventy weeks were, to some, actually seventy counts of seven. And since 'seven' would mean a week, this would be interpreted as 70 weeks prophesy. Without further ado to, let's say the 70-year exile of the Old Testament, let us find our way back to "three."

It is evident that to mend the ones who lost track and put the broken in perspective, the time chosen was not 1 month, 1 year, the harvest; it was "seven."

Advance 6 and rest 1.

This was the measure; Shabbat was the measure.

Pause and rest before hard work turns into lust, enthusiasm into recklessness, achievement into heist. Not because you cannot go on without resting; but because you cannot have a command of yourself if you do not pause.

Shabbat taught me about 3.

3, in turn, is about "pause:" to learn to pause.

It is two of us again. We know it cannot be changed once given; the name that is… That is why we will whisper it neatly and gently.

We will know the name; but will not share.

This is the name of the girl who carries the wisdom into the dreams. We will draw will and power from her, and in turn, we will protect her as the priceless treasure she is.

This name will give us the courage to dream; and we will not shiver, we will not blush when we come to the crossing roads to wisdom.

She will be our beacon of light.

I am truly grateful that we encountered the Book of Daniel while looking for this formidable light.

This is what I learned this Saturday: Just like I need that courage to get up when I stumble when walking or tumble when running or have a fresh start to hang on, I need to learn how to pause. And surely, the understanding of when to do which.

And there is no such thing as to work nonstop, with no rest. Or that the life would stop if you do. With no exception, everyone, but everyone, needs to press the pause button. Even when the prophets pass on, the religions endure; and life goes on. We shall all stop and rest in this sacred continuation.

Except the Angels… They do not hang onto time as we do, so they do not need to pause. But me, you, us: we do.

In the:

Past

Present

and

Future.

Count to 1, 2, 3: And we need to learn to halt: to curb the greed, pause the life, and say "fermata."

Maritime Hotel, New York ~

Klara got settled in the pizzeria on the ground floor of the Maritime Hotel as discussed. The weather was absolutely gorgeous, and it was a great idea to sit outside in the courtyard. The stairs from the street lead right into the yard so it was a perfect spot to wait and watch the crowd pass by. The waiter almost instantly appeared by her side, which nearly made her utter a few words of complaint, but the mood completely changed as he asked her if she was Miss Klara.

"Yes, I'm Klara," she replied.

"You have a package for the publishing house, I understand," the waiter said. "May I have it if it's ready?"

She reached for the large yellow envelope in her bag without a word. Then, after a few seconds of hesitation, she decided to order a ginger Schnapps as she handed over the envelope.

She was a little upset. She had on a nice spring dress and her hair was elegantly pulled back. That knitted jacket on her shoulders felt like an unnecessary garment all of a sudden. She placed it on the chair beside her; she was overheated. What was she expecting?

"What the heck!" she mumbled. "I should go ahead and have a nice feast anyway. I *am* here after all, am I not?" She ordered a salad with blue cheese and walnuts as a starter and then an arugula & prosciutto pizza. She thought she might even order a glass of chardonnay with the pizza.

She had nothing to read and pass the time other than the tabloid she had been handed at the subway entrance. She browsed the pages as she sipped the Schnapps. It was a perfect day to just watch people go by and daydream, and she was going to do exactly that. After a while, she dreamt herself in that movie "You've Got Mail." Just like Meg Ryan, unaware of being watched over by Tom Hanks at the Café Lalo, Klara was ready to leave when she felt a tap on her shoulder.

"I was at one of those tables in the back. I didn't want to miss meeting you, Klara."

Klara recognized the voice as that of Jan Gregorev. She hesitated to start on a first-name basis. The guy wasn't around her age, but he was definitely much younger than she had thought. She took a deep breath to calm her nerves because he was also gorgeously handsome.

"Pleasure," she said, holding out her hand.

"How about a walk in the park? It's really a nice day outside," he replied as he took her hand.

As she agreed, she quickly reckoned that they were on 15th Street and he just suggested a walk in Central Park. 'So, we will walk to 60th Street now?' she thought to herself.

"I would like to go over 'Three' together. And this deserves a good, long walk in my book," he said. Klara felt as if he must have read her mind. They crossed from 9th Avenue to 8th, and they began to walk all the way up to 58th Street to the Park entrance.

"Years ago, I learned something from a street artist in Montreal," said Gregorev, as they started their journey. "My initial goal was to dust off my French as I started to hold a conversation with him. But then it got a little more interesting. We chatted for a bit. Finally, he gave me his email to send him a picture of the painting I bought after it had been framed and hung. He was full of the anticipation of documenting the exhibit of his work by a guy – me – whose original intention was only to tune up his poor French. But, you see, all artists, writers, painters wish their work to be recognized, authenticated, framed, and presented. Surely, your standpoint cannot be any different?"

"There's been a new discovery in an excursion site in Egypt; perhaps you've heard?" said Klara, now deciding to continue this conversation more informally. It was *her* work that they were talking about. She had to be in the right state of mind and focus on the things that were to be discussed. She was not going to let courtly manners get in the way, nor would she allow this beautiful man to dominate the conversation. She organized her thoughts and focused so that she was ready for the battle of words. Jan Gregorev could not have possibly known it, but this was her strong suit. "Ready handsome?" she thought. "I'm not just a pretty face. *En guard!*"

Klara was ready to bring it out. "One of the mummies found in that excavation belonged to a long-forgotten prince. The findings brought out the fact that contrary to the arguments the archaeologists have been claiming, this prince had not died as a coward; it was almost a miracle that he lived the life he did considering how sick he was! Now, I'm not sure if the historians will go back to alter their perspectives about that era; but at least they will need to bring some explanation to clarify this last finding. You see, that prince was not an artist. But his last piece of work was to have his corpse lying down to be found. Perhaps that corpse even struggled to be unearthed in the mysterious world of Egypt.

To shed light onto the unknown, to correct the records, to give hope to one who needs it… It is crucial that a work of achievement should not be left in the dusty corners. To pass on the knowledge - the correct knowledge - no matter how small, onto thousands or even to one person perhaps, to hand over the baton, to make record of what is proven by history, and to share this with the world? Yes, I'm in favor of preserving and passing on this kind of work, even if not framed and hung on a wall."

A little astonished, Gregorev watched Klara, who finished her words with a sigh of relief yet with amusement. Could it be that he had finally found his match of a swordsman? He unexpectedly changed the subject in the hopes of baffling her.

"Tell me about that Saturday when you wrote about "three." It was really on Saturday, wasn't it?" he asked.

"Yes," smiled Klara. "But it was three Saturdays in a row. I was looking for a sign. And it came with the Book of Daniel. A friend of mine was going to weekly Bible studies and she coincidentally started to tell me about it. The Book of Daniel started to resonate all of a sudden. The Book of Daniel… The Book of Daniel… At first it may look like the conclusion, when actually it was the beginning and the climax.

Things started to have more perspective when I realized that those "seventy weeks" were not weeks but a "group of seven" or a "unit of time." When I linked this to the creation in seven units of time, Shabbat had a new meaning for me. Then I took it from there to talk about when to stop and when to go on. Shabbat meant to 'pause' and was going to be my approach."

Klara felt that she was riding her mustang, and all the winds were behind her. It didn't seem likely that she could be jousted down.

Did Gregorev hope otherwise? Absolutely not and he would hand it to her. But, not just yet. He would hustle her a bit further, and like it or not he would resort to ridicule.

"So, would you say the angels helped?" he countered with an self-satisfied smirk on his face.

"Jan Gregorev!" She picked it up. "And the inevitable question… My exchange with the angels started just like this: By climbing all over those who believed. It took a long time as I moved from disbelief to suspicion, then to being not-so-ambivalent and putting things to small tests, until I finally believed. Just like those who walk this path, I've started to find feathers in the most curious places at unexpected times and started to interpret the startling shapes of clouds. Then one day - it was my birthday - they dazzled me with a surprise. After all that intrigue, we started with a new white, a wondrous page.

To make it short, I woke up in the middle of the night with music. My computer was on and a rhapsody I love was playing. First, I was very scared, but then, I loved it. I am sure there are many other ways to explain why the rhapsody started to play all of a sudden. But I chose to accept this as the angels' way of giving me a birthday present. You need to understand that they are very cheerful and amusing. Otherwise, would they quietly make you stand up from where you were sitting at the Maritime and give you this surprise?"

"Which surprise?" asked Gregorev. He was trying to relate to what he was hearing. When he looked down from where they were standing, he saw the Bethesda

Fountain. In this prominent spot of the Central Park, the fountain was adorned with an angel on top. The Bethesda Angel was offering his hands to Gregorev and was almost blinking while asking him to join this game.

Gregorev gently put his arms up accepting his defeat and smiled.

"And you are not going to say 'no' especially to an angel who is there to purify something you like so much, 'the water,' will you now?" asked Klara.

She was enjoying her little triumph. She wasn't the one who wanted to take a walk this way. "It's the Angels' doing," she added. "They've always been good to me. If you let them in and give them some space in your life, I'm sure they will do the same for you. And don't be shy to accept the blessings they offer."

They both knew this was the end of the conversation and the stroll. As he reached into his pockets for some papers, he found that it was his turn to surprise her. "I am looking forward to what you will write in 'four.' And I want you to have these – what I wrote in 'five' – years ago. We will have a lot to talk about next time we meet," he said.

As they said goodbye, he had to fight the urge to give her a kiss. He could almost feel Mrs. Simi's shadow looking down from her apartment. "Silly," he thought. "It's not even facing this side of the Park." As he was about to turn away, the most unexpected thing happened when Klara leaned in to give him a kiss on one cheek.

"As they do in Europe," she said. "I wanted to thank you for this beautiful afternoon."

Then Gregorev did something he had not done for the longest time. He planted a little kiss on Klara's hand. "As they do in Europe," he said.

Four ~

Honor thy father and thy mother

I'm calling on Archangel Uriel. To give me light, to show me the way as I assemble a sanctorum from words. I am trying to build this with some from here, some from there with earth, water, fire, and wind. Will I be able to put a roof atop of four walls when there is so much mystery to solve? Will I be able to crack into the unknown of moving from the triangle to the square? Please be my light, Archangel Uriel; be my guide to understand what I see when I start looking inside.

Four is the number of creation; Completeness and wholeness with Sun and the Moon.

Four directions…

Four winds…

Four seasons…

It is stability.

Steadiness…

The foundation…

But before anything else, it is family, togetherness. It is the aggregation that holds the mother, the father, and the child.

If there needed be a number to transform the power of creation into matter, it would be "four." Then the paths would be opened, and the ideas crowned.

And it is the number of Jupiter, the symbol of the protector and justice.

It is said that if you see the number four over and over again, know that the angels are with you and behind you, waiting for you to ask for guidance, should you be unaware of your capability and power.

The little girl was keeping a close watch on the lady with the straw hat through the white fence under the massive maple tree to see what was going on in the neighboring garden. The fence was high; it wasn't possible for her to look and see anything over it. But surely she could find a good spot from in between to catch a nice, comfortable viewpoint. Her grandpa could certainly grow those as well, but he always liked the flowers more. Next door, cherry tomatoes, sweet smelling strawberries, clusters of grapes, and many more fruits and vegetables were starting to ripen alongside the blossoming flowers.

She was watching the straw-hat woman so intensely that she was startled when she heard a voice from the opposite side.

"Have you ever heard of a sea creature called the mantis shrimp?" asked the boy next door.

"No," she replied, "What are they like?"

"They can see multiples of what humans see as colors. While humans have three sensors in their eyes, they have twelve! Think about it. They can see four times the colors than we do!"

The little girl got up on her toes. She still wasn't able to see over the fence. Now the boy did the same. He must have been taller because his eyes were visible over the hedge.

"I'm saying f-o-u-r times! This must be incredible."

She pointed at her grandpa's flowers while forcing her imagination. "You mean there are more colors in these flowers than that we can see?"

"And can you believe into how many more colors these already colorful peppers will turn? I would like to see that," he said with a know-it-all tone. After a slight hesitation, he looked at the little girl and asked, "Their buds are really small. Would you like to see them?"

The little girl didn't want to be seen to be too enthusiastic, but it was too late. She accepted the invitation with a cheerful reply. "I'd like that very much. But I have to ask my grandpa first," she said as she was half-way there.

She was at the neighbor's door right away. With the taller boy, they went to see the pepper buds. That's when she realized that the straw-hat woman was much younger than she thought. Her cheerful garden gloves were covered in soil. She told the little girl to get comfortable in the chair in the shade after a quick tour of the basil, rosemary, and thyme.

She came back with long glasses with thin stems in her hand. "Would you like to taste our mint ice tea?" The little girl politely took an involuntary sip from this unknown cold drink and looked *at the hostess with a huge surprise in her eyes. The woman with the straw hat now resting next to her smiled easily and clarified the mystery of this scrumptious mixture by identifying it as lemon thyme and honey.*

There was no sign of the boy who went inside to find some pictures of the mantis shrimp.

"Which ones are your favorite plants?" she asked the woman, while taking more sips of the minty goodness.

"Hyacinth, daffodil, and of course the tulips in spring time… Then lilac and the magnolia…Did I mention peonies? Followed by the roses, surely. We have nice variety of roses in our garden. Each one more fragrant and charming than the next. When the hydrangeas start to blossom, the spring will be over; but the pansies, marigolds, and begonias will decorate the garden. The tomatoes will turn red, the peppers will grow pointed and the grapes will hang down from the trellis. This is the celebration of nature. Shouldn't miss a minute of it…"

"But what about when winter comes?" the girl asked. "When everything is covered with snow, do you get sad and give up?" The little girl was totally at ease in her chair, nibbling on gingersnaps.

"Not a chance," said the woman with absolute certainty. "Even if my heart fails, my mind would not allow it. Because I know the life will continue in its cycles. In a few months, we will start all over again and celebrate life with colors, scents, and flavors. This gives me the strength to go on.

Once upon a time, I held in my arms a tiny little newborn who opened his eyes to this world way earlier than he was due. Oh, how he was striving to hold on to life with his frail fingers with almost no nails. I would say I was born again after knowing him. That teeny-weeny body with that itty-bitty wrinkled face had a huge heart and a sharp consciousness that wouldn't let go. Life is so precious, yet we do not always appreciate it as much as those who newly open their eyes to it.

I feel embarrassed to give up every time I remember the way he clung to life. I know that tiny being is the one who stimulated to love and protect the life within me; the mother and the father. And perhaps that is why I want to be present every time the nature awakens.

The mother in us is the soul: and the father, the wisdom.

I celebrate life at every chance the nature offers it and so honor the mother and the father."

The woman stopped talking.

She was amazed at herself for telling all these things to the little girl on this summer day. She wasn't sure if the little girl had even listened to her let alone grasped what she said. She felt a little discomfited.

The dense air cleared with the boy's sudden and loud burst from the house.

"Can you believe this?" he asked, holding the mantis shrimp pictures in his hand. "I just read that they don't actually see all these colors. They can perceive them, but not see them. What do you think they do with all those colors they are aware of but can't see?" he asked the little girl.

The little girl hopped down from the chair she was sitting at. "I think they may have a telepathic connection with those colors.

But we will never know this, will we?" She approached the boy wisely.

Then she thanked the straw-hat woman for the beautiful time spent together knowing that her grandpa would like her to do it that way.

And before she left, again in that wise manner, she looked at the tall boy and said, "Only a tiny being like that would get to know the mantis shrimps this well," and left the woman sitting open-mouthed, the straw hat held tightly in her hand.

Dear Archangel Uriel,

When you offered me a hug and a place in the timelessness of thousand years, I realized that honoring the mother and father is not about coddling them.

To glorify them, one needs to search other gardens; take a journey within and connect with soul and mind.

Completeness, wholeness, steadiness and foundation will only then make sense.

In that timelessness you offered me, I built a tiny sanctorum with four walls; with stones from my heart and stones from my mind.

I have gotten to know what "to love," "to protect," "to guide," and "to fight" mean all over.

I understood once again what "mother" and "father" stand for.

And I've done this with my soul and my mind.

So, I am forever grateful.

Thank you.

***

"Soul and mind… Mother and Father…" muttered Mr. Oliver. He of course was reading a copy of these essays. The "mind and soul" that came along with "four" reminded him of the "mother and father" they left back in Europe with Rosa. He was never the one to express his choices out loud, perhaps, due to his circumstances. But now he could confess – at least to himself – that he was leaning towards sympathy when Klara was in question and he might even want to get to know her better.

Mr. Oliver ~~

It was no other than Mr. Oliver who was pacing up and down the apartment viewing Central Park. He was taking those unwavering steps almost to reassure the safe passage of time of those never-ending three-week intervals. Time was of the essence and they would need more of it to prepare these two people on their list for the job should their plans fall into place as hoped. Time, time, time! This *was* a scarcity. Was Mrs. Simi aware of it? At this age, trying to pin the candidates, trips to Europe and all that evaluation meetings were wearing him down. He really would like to retire at this point and spend his time – let's see – having tea and sandwiches all day perhaps.

A long, long time ago, it happened that Mr. Oliver became the trustee of a group of gentlemen's secrets from Europe. The South of France had hosted many immigrants after the Great War. A group of them were royals with diminished wealth and visionaries in search of innovations. It was the time when socialism and communism were about to take the place of imperialism and capitalism. A great change was on the doorstep of Europe. Empires were taken over by the smaller sovereign states and a way of life was coming to an end.

New political and social waves were rolling in. A handful people who saw the first signs were already worrying about the future. They almost knew the Second World War was approaching and held few hopes if any for what would come after. Among them were many brilliant people with a broad command of arts, science, literature, and philosophy.

Ollie was just a little boy then. A boy with no awareness of the plans the future had for him. A part of his family had already immigrated to the United States. Knowing this, Grandfather Gregorev with a group of others chose this promising child and prepared him to go to America. Needless to say, they were not only group of intellectuals in Europe. Just like the Gregorev's group assembled in South France, others were gathering in different cities and countries to make the most of the findings and knowledge they held. It was rumored that another group in Italy had focused on self-interest rather than social advancement. Not everyone was acting with precaution of course; for some "war" meant "jeopardy," and for others, it was "fortune."

The group in South France was fairly at ease. Perhaps they would never go back to the luxury of their earlier lives, but they had enough means to comfortably get by and this was secured by those solid investments they had made. Nobody could do this like the Swiss, and no war would change that. Their wealth and future were entrusted to the Swiss and Mr. Oliver reassured himself that this was not a bad decision. All those advances and investments made through the years were thanks to the wise decisions taken in Europe years before.

The choices that had been made and the decisions taken were not limited to investments. The wise men of the Old World also decided to send a girl to America together with Ollie. Rosa was a gifted, smart, and promising choice. Their families were both visionaries and only distantly related: those marriages that would keep them so were all a part of the past. Rosa was the first girl to be trusted with this kind of a responsibility. Her father used to call her "my shining eastern star." The handful of intellectuals trusting their decisions graciously equipped these two young people to see them off to the United States.

Rosa and Ollie chose new family names in the New World. Ollie became Mr. Oliver; Rosa, Mrs. Simi. Their years-long friendship did not turn into anything else. They both had relations, none of which ended up with marriage. It wouldn't be reasonable to expect otherwise with the kind of turbulent lives they were leading. They were fully occupied with all those mind-blowing inventions, innovations, and advances that had to be managed. Finally, when they took a pause and confessed that they had advanced in age, they settled in the two-story apartment overlooking the park.

The apartment was so big that they decided to move in together. Nobody knew that they were not married.

They might have forgotten it themselves. One in the lower and the other on the second floor, they were two very old and good friends with a fulfilling life. They could play a hand of pinochle during those long winter nights and perhaps occasionally accompany one another to a concert.

Besides, neither Mr. Oliver's sandwiches nor Mrs. Simi's teas would taste the same when alone. Although they had abundant means, they didn't have live-in help. Maybe in the years to come this would be a must, but for now it was unnecessary. They had assistance in the house all day long, and also at their offices. Surely, they could never be able to explain this to Mrs. Kenwood. Even if they did, she wouldn't understand – well, she wouldn't want to understand, anyway.

It was not for nothing that he thought of Kenwood. Because no matter how much they discussed the matter, it wasn't legally possible to seal the deal without the consent of Rosa's cousin Hilda Kenwood and last but not least, Jacque Arlo.

"First things first," he thought. He had to take care of business with Mr. Aziz before anything else. He went downstairs to see Mrs. Simi.

"This must be serious since you came down with tawny port in your hand," said Mrs. Simi.

"I thought a little sweet wine wouldn't hurt," he said as he offered one glass to her. "Rosa…" he continued,

"I see how content you seem with Jan Gregorev and Klara. But we also need an eagle and a crow."

"A crow?" asked Mrs. Simi.

"Well, I wanted to emphasize it with a smart bird, I suppose. You know, crows are the smartest of birds," he said.

"What about you? Do you see Jan and Klara as the right couple?" asked Mrs. Simi, still wondering about his choice of the crow.

"Fairly," answered Mr. Oliver. "But you know as well as I do that we need to decide on the other two no matter how good they play their fair share of our choice. We have to start preparing the reinforcing team of two, backing the front runners, who will be in more plain sight. Just like in our times."

"Reinforcements? Like Hilda Kenwood?" sighed Mrs. Simi. She couldn't decide if she preferred the crow or Hilda.

***

About around the same time in another part of the town, Klara was in her chair thinking with her papers on the opposite corner. Actually, what was keeping her mind busy was not much different that of Mr. Oliver's, whom she had never met before: The "change." Although for different reasons; both were very intrigued with things not being the way they used to be.

Klara didn't know how to explain it. Perhaps this is the way she was feeling now that it was time for "five." Five was the number of "change," and "change" was not and could not possibly be better or worse. Every new step would open doors to different paths of fate. And, that is why it couldn't be worse. Yet, not everything would go well with that first step: At the very least of it, it would not be all well-received easily. Some things would change with "5." And perhaps, it was time. Wasn't her relation with Jan also different now? During these past weeks, words had become a cozy hideaway for them both and they were comfortable cuddling beneath it. She had read what Jan wrote in "5" and sensed that he had somehow encountered death, or at least hastily wandered around it. That handsome and distantly arrogant guy had a heart touched by grief and loss. Klara shook off the impulse to touch that heart and wrote a little note at the end before she mailed out her last piece.

***

Jan,

It was really nice of you to share your writing with me. I do not know if you ever expected this; but I decided to combine our works knowing that you like to be pleasantly surprised. In the next piece, until after the end of the "dream," it is my "five." Then, your "five" will follow. It is an odd feeling to get together to write about death. As if we walked through it together... Hope you will enjoy.

Klara

P.S. I actually had that dream.

For Mr. Oliver, things were a little bit more complicated. He was aware that the winds had changed course. This, stronger than a feeling, was more of an awareness. He knew all very well at this age that it was not easy to prevail against strong winds. But he also knew this; if you do not fight them and instead turn to corral those fierce gusts at your back, you could conquer the world. And with Rosa, this is exactly what they would do; they would be sure to have those winds at their backs.

Five ~~

Thou shall not kill

I'm calling on Archangel Azrael. Quietly. Please be a comfort to all those who have lost their loved ones. Ease their pain. Know that their tears are not shed for nothing. Breathe a little compassion and some solace into their hearts. It really is burdensome to be left behind, especially to be apart with peace of mind. It is really hard to say good bye even if the passing away is natural and timely. It is harder when death comes from accidents, murders, or those incidents where there is no closure because the remains cannot be found. I am praying that you will touch those grieving souls; touch them so the passage is a little easier. Life is there alongside death. You may be born; but once you are, you will surely die.

All the questions about death are harsh; but those about "killing" are much more hard-hitting. Dark shadows pass along my eyes. I am trying to avoid the hardest questions with dread after I say, "Thou shall not kill," because I know... There exist thousands of disgraceful examples that can be blamed on humans and humanity once you start asking, "Wouldn't you?"

"Five" is the number of people.

One head.

Two arms,

Two legs,

Five.

Five fingers on a hand.

The left hand is a silhouette of a human; so is the right. And when you put those two together, isn't it the same as a prayer?

Humans feel.

Humans think.

It is that human on top that holds the pyramid together, with its four walls on the sides.

Five is human; five is humanity.

It is our number, "five." We have five senses; the sixth is only a sensation.

It is our figure, "the pentagon." When you join the ends together; the circle becomes eternity. But this is for later… After-death later…

Before all else, what makes us human is our wisdom. If it was not for wisdom, like the four winds blowing away on their own, four elements being their own master, and four seasons with their own states of mind, we humans would be scattered apart.

Every April, we humans, we revive.

This is deliverance.

Humans take in a breath as the first step into life.

The first breath is taken, not given, perhaps because there is nothing to give. There is no breath to give. And when it is time to part, that first breath is given as the last.

In some cultures, breath is called "soul;" this is perhaps the way they part with the body together at last.

Breath, it is… When touching the blood, it bears life. It is not up to you or me to make it stop.

Not an animal's, not a plant's, let alone a human life is ours to end. That is perhaps why they say, "ask nature's permission when you are about to pick a flower."

And surely, we should be grateful for that breath we take, that we wake up with the opportunity to take another.

Otherwise, death is close by, in the reach of a hand.

Once you enter the valley of life, how is it possible to know how far you have to travel? How is it ever possible to know the end? You may taste it many times but swallow it once. Once you do, there is no turning back. No one returns from that point.

***

It is a cool April night and I know I am in a dream. I know this because I am accompanied by those who I laid down six feet under and who have then risen to the heavens above. As I walk through this dream, I am wondering how far I can go... Who I will see... What I will witness... What it is that's written for me to live in this dream...

Those who are standing next to me are family that we bade farewell long ago. They introduce me to her.

For a split second this doesn't suit me well.

Short black hair and blue eyes... This is what I recall. Also, that she is a young woman of fair height.

She can read everyone's past and future.

"She will tell you what will happen with one single touch," they say.

"She will tell me the future," I assume.

Not a second later, she lightly touches me — and this is because I am not fast enough to move away- from her index finger. This subtle touch stimulates all my nerves. Right then, I collect myself to withdraw. I am bewildered because I never wanted to meet her this way. And I find myself feeling naïve and helpless that I am not prepared for it. Almost ignorant... What was I expecting when I knowingly walked into a dream this adrift, this insecure? Was she going to show me her real face to trap me?

She takes advantage as I falter and grabs my arm.

Electrified, I start shattering.

I start wondering if one can die in the realm of dreams if they are electrified? I had been shocked and shattered in a dream before; which one is stronger? I try to compare. All this happens in a split second or perhaps even less than that. And I suddenly realize she is still holding my arm. It can't be more that a second, I feel; otherwise dream or not I could not possibly still be alive.

Her bloodshot eyes radiate in blue.

Her face shape-shifts.

Her black hair is now a thorn bush encircling her face.

And the face takes the color of a metal smelting in flames.

Those eyes are now a piercing blue.

Can anyone standing next to me see her? Or is she showing herself only to me?

The moment I realize that there is no one beside me, I let loose the scream stuck in my throat to wake myself up.

As she says, "I finally found you," through closed lips, she looks at me with a treacherous smile. I hear her voice resonating in my brain for a while after she disappears…

***

My body is stiff; very stiff.

I open my eyes and think

That this is a dream…

That the life and death that manifest beyond our physical body is not much different from the one within.

That you cannot even for a second close your third eye…

And that death, pointlessly or just like a game, can capture you with fake bait.

Five is the number of people.

Close your eyes and trust me.

Extend from your heart that left arm.

Hang on to life while you have time, purely and deservedly.

When the day comes, take one resolute step with your right foot into the realm of light.

Meet your end with honor and integrity.

I surely wouldn't wish for you to be one of those unfortunates who fall a slave to purgatory.

Erratically hanging down with that right hand; don't try to hold onto life when the end is there.

Because, I, Jan Gregorev, have met the men who fell for purgatory. This is a childhood story: it is not a flattering one, but it is a true story.

I had not seen many people drowning in their tears. That is probably why I had my eyes wide open trying to grasp the depth of what was going on.

Not without fear but — let's say — with a fair amount of bravado, I approached the man.

It was raining fiercely, and the fresh smell of the soil was prevalent. In weather like this, the guy at the old house was known to drag his scrawny father into the woods and place him on the rocky altar to perform a ritual of unfamiliar chanting. It was one of those nights.

He was soaking beneath his tears as he was rubbing down the skin and bones that remained of his father, trying to revive the old man with the rhythmic chanting. The words leaving his mouth were most eerie. "Pserken inaska niirt."

Was he not in control of his tongue? Or did these words have a meaning that I could not comprehend?

"Nayerkt anzuka biirt," he continued.

I looked around to see if there were any more curious eyes where I was hunkered down.

There were none.

I moved closer.

It was all about the skeletal body for the son; nothing else mattered.

As I walked towards him, I said, "It is as if you are begging the skies so the secrets can come down and find you." I continued, "I do not understand what you are chanting but I'm sure they are hiding a secret, because only words embedded with secrets sound like this."

He didn't care. It was as if he had to recite all the chants before the night was over. He was in a hurry.

The son had been trying for a long time to divert this skeletal body, from its inevitable path. He had given his promise to the father, after all, when he was instructed, "Do not let me go."

What the son did not understand was that trying to block the path of the father was not the way to honor him. What if he tried to prolong the journey with some rotten chants from the old black books? When the contract is over, they will come and get him.

But I couldn't have known this back then.

I was young.

Nevertheless, all this really happened.

And more importantly, I pray that you would be spared to be one of the living dead: Alive but thankful that "another hour is over," having the left leg caught in a life where the soul is tormented, and the body is raped; breathing but dead.

Because, I, Jan Gregorev, have met those who were already dead when alive… I have listened to them rise from the dead and this is their story. It is not pleasant, but it is true.

Her childhood was shattered. every single night... at her own house…The place she knew as home…On the bed where she was supposed to sleep…There was no such bed…It was that brutal. Even if she folded her body into a ceaseless cry, there was no shelter to take. Not a drop of strength to look for a relief for her body was crippled by fear. Perhaps, death? Ending this life? Taking his life? But she was young, so very young, and her arms and legs were so frail... Every night, as she pretended to be asleep, she prayed that "that night, hopefully, she would just die."

Then, in her teens, the ferocious fire in her was so fierce that hellfire seemed innocent. She created a story of dancing with the devil. A little of it was her desperation, but mostly it was her way to get back at them; to make it up for what she had lived through... All she wanted to do was to torture her body... At least she could be in control of it now. That's how she tried to get even. As the sun went down, she would drug herself before hitting the street; men or women; it didn't matter. Screams would rise behind the solid door, but no one heard, and no one cared. Until the sunrise, the noise would go on. In the morning, she would try to mend her body, but not her soul. Her soul would not heal that easily.

This other girl; she was trying to escape death. She would talk so effortlessly that one would know that she really had been through all this and that it was all true. It was mind-blowing how death stalked her all those years. She knew, with all those accidents, they could not be bizarre and repulsive coincidences. Mostly, she was worried about her loved ones. What if it started to chase them too? Wherever she went, she would see it and carry it along with her.

"To give up," she would say, "was a sweet sensation. And I so wanted to taste it. It would be very easy for me, like having a charming drink." She really did want to let go... "Just once? Please?"

There are those who lost nails, shed hair, and were covered in bruises. Some came to be almost blind, and toothless at best. There

*are those who cannot stand up, and those who cannot lie down…
In the corners, on the floor waiting for hours in darkness… Have
you ever seen the body rocking back and forth, just like that sitting
down; lying in bed… Nothing to be heard; nothing to be seen…
Back, and forth, back and forth… When you think it is fatal,
pray for Azrail to come forth. But, it does not happen. If it does
not happen, it does not happen.*

*And then, when it is least expected, they stand up. Soul
purified, wound healed, leg started to mend, and those empty eyes
almost shine with a sudden spark. The scale decides to favor life
over death.*

You see, when there is still time, there is still time.

*I have met more than one of those who defied the ashes. I have
to say that they are stronger than the strongest. First, their strength
is still. That confidence of being competent is not a mouthful to
gulp down. They enjoy it in silent bites.*

*I have learned, if nothing else, from those who did not deserve
to die and, if it was up to you and me, about those who deservedly
did:*

Death cannot be rushed.

Everyone, but everyone, has that price to pay.

*The price is to be paid by him who caused it; and will be
collected by the one who suffered it…. This price, although
seldomly settled between those two, never goes without being paid.*

Thou shall not kill.

Because in return, the one who has a price to pay has to live through whatever he needs to live through before, during, and at the time of his death.

And, I, Jan Gregorev, beyond all, wish to maintain a clear head.

Never forget, it is not up to you or me to decide the terms.

You cannot enter in the middle of the game.

Let what is to be lived, be lived through. Even at death.

Mr. Aziz ∿

They were in an area in New Jersey populated with immigrants from the Balkans. As they drove on Route 4 after crossing the George Washington Bridge, they almost found themselves in another world. They did not talk much on the way except to go over some talking points for the meeting that was about to happen.

Now they were at Mr. Aziz's house and welcomed into the tea room. The dining table, covered with a handmade lace tablecloth, was adorned with mouth-watering delicacies. *Small pitas, bourekas – both Albanian and Skopje style – homemade ajvar, thin slices of soujouk and kashkaval cheese, cookies, krempita and samsa were all arrayed in an eye pleasing display. Traditional tea glasses suggested that tea would be served in the Turkish style. (*Pita=flat bread, bourekas=stuffed puff pastry pockets, ajvar=red pepper relish, soujouk=sausage, krempita=custard slices, samsa=type of a dumpling)

Mr. Aziz was, as always, very gracious as he welcomed the guests. Mrs. Simi was very sincere when she said, "You went through a lot of trouble with this preparation for us," as she shook hands with Mr. Aziz.

"Only because this is the afternoon tea. Otherwise, if you could stay for dinner, we would also have lamb chops," Mr. Aziz said. "You know Katrina. She can't feel good about it otherwise."

"I hope she can join us," said Mrs. Simi.

"Absolutely," Mr. Aziz confirmed. "She will join us for tea."

"Dear Aziz. You know I am not here to play chess with you today. There are some issues we need to discuss," Mr. Oliver wanted to get this conversation started, while Mrs. Simi observed Mr. Aziz.

The two had met when Mr. Aziz was busy organizing several Balkan associations to hold some joint cultural activities, which would overlap with some ventures that Mr. Oliver was undertaking. He was a watch repairman, a patient one. He was also a self-disciplined, coordinated, and well-trusted friend. Additionally, Aziz was a marbling artist.

Mrs. Simi couldn't but wonder if he was a reed player. "If so, he is the perfect dervish," she thought. He had his share of that culture, nonetheless, and this was a very important nuance.

In his younger years, while still living in Macedonia, he had fallen in love with an Albanian girl. The everlasting love between him and his wife Katrina had blossomed in the old lands. Their marriage was built upon tolerance. Aziz would fast during Ramadan and Katrina would decorate the tree at Christmas. There was no question that both of their families had unfavorable views at the time and did try to undermine this marriage. But the young couple would lean on each other and survived the test of time. Finally, because of their determination and by sweetly making their way into each other's families, the couple received everyone's blessing.

In the early years of their marriage, they had to make hard choices, just like many families did in the Balkans., Back in the 1980's and the end of Cold War, Aziz tried to make a living at many jobs, but he was unable to make ends meet for his family. Finally, he had to accept that the opportunities were growing really weak in Eastern Europe. To build his future, he would rather go to America than Western Europe.

Ethnic groups in the Balkans were going through an awakening after the iron claw of the Soviets was suddenly lifted off them. Yugoslavia would be replaced by several sovereign states. Communism that ruled this area since WWII intimidated the dervishes and the practice of Sufism that had survived in the region for many centuries. It seemed that it would then almost face extinction. Almost, but not likely! Eren men knew how to withdraw and keep to themselves in order to survive. Associations would legally vanish, but families would carry on in secret with their traditions. Belonging to one of these families, Aziz had a natural training in hiding and guarding the writings, the costumes, and the original treasures. While immigrating to America, he had brought along these treasures, and made an invaluable contribution to the preservation and continuity of this culture. Mr. Oliver knew all about these.

"I am listening," said Mr. Aziz to Mrs. Simi and Mr. Oliver with a tranquility reserved for those who confidently try to bear the past and carry it into the future.

"Long before you, we also brought along some very valuable things from Europe," said Mr. Oliver, looking over as Mrs. Simi picked up the conversation again.

"Limited edition and rare books, manuscripts, scientific findings, and so on. But these were only the tip of the iceberg. For many years, explorations, innovations just short of miracles were piled up and meticulously guarded in Europe. These contained knowledge that belonged to the future. And it is simply because the technology was not sufficient at the time to bring them to light. Some were philosophical approaches that needed to wait for people to advance. These were 'future' and had they come out at the wrong time, they would do nothing but raise questions. They may even have ended up being thrown on a fire and being destroyed or willingly handed over to looters or used for a witch hunt. Our mission was to keep them safe until the world and humanity had progressed enough to be ready for these treasures to come out."

He paused a little. He wondered how Mr. Aziz was taking all this in. After all, this could easily be seen as a fictitious mind game that two old people were making up. However, Mr. Aziz did not look like he found the conversation all that odd.

Mr. Oliver continued. "Now, it is time to hand the responsibility over to the next generation. Although we have materialized some of them, there is much that is still waiting for the right time. Let's just say we are trying to prepare a vanguard of two people to shepherd our treasure to the science and philosophy communities. We are here because we want you to be the reinforcement, together with another candidate, to be guardians of this enormous wealth. Before you say anything, we'd like you to know that you can take your time to think about it."

"Although I did not have a chance to get to know you as well as Mr. Oliver, I also do believe that you be most suitable for the job," said Mrs. Simi. "Should you agree, we will be honored."

"It's as if I knew this day would come," said Mr. Aziz as he started to talk again. "It wasn't just the quality of our chess meets that made me feel close to you and respect you. I always appreciated your work, your view of life. And during those occasional opportunities that we had to work together, I might have secretly hoped for more to come.

As you know, I try to bring various Balkan associations together when an occasion arises. This is because in essence, I believe people from similar backgrounds tend to avoid conflict when opportunities emerge to envelop them all and also when they remember what they mutually share. Simply put, I've seen that the Bosnian, the Croatian, the Slav, the Albanian, the Thracian all eat those dolmades that are cooked in every kitchen all the way from Aegean into the depths of Balkans with same spirit yet simplicity. That is why I started to try bringing people together with some cultural events. One of the two of my best aids is Sufism and the other is challenging dinner tables. I do know that this is a bit too much of a good faith, and perhaps utopia. But then again, when you advance to more serious subjects, the meals once shared always help to break the ice. And we did come a long way like that."

He paused and then continued with the same serenity that he had demonstrated throughout the conversation. "I will continue to work with good will and compassion for all humanity. Hence, I am honored by your offer. And I will work to make it worthwhile as long as I physically can and with the time I have remaining on this earth." But, he was not done. "Yet, I will have one condition," he said, looking at Mr. Oliver and Mrs. Simi. "I have always walked these paths together with Katrina. She will need to know." He was now done. The rest were details.

Mr. Oliver and Ms. Simi barely looked at each other. Everything had gone much easier and smoother than they had anticipated. They were grateful. They nodded in confirmation. Katrina joined them with her immaculate timing. She placed a platter of warm turnovers that the neighbors sent. She started a conversation with her soothing voice. Aziz and Katrina were a couple liked and respected by people living closely in peace and bonded to one another. Aziz and Katrina were the right choice.

***

When Mrs. Simi and Mr. Oliver reached their park view apartment, now a heavy weight lifted off of their shoulders, they would never think that certain developments that took place simultaneously with their initiative would blow them to a different venue all together. The surprise of the night was a note that Jacques Arlo had sent.

I suppose it is "hand over" time. It is unbelievable how quickly the years pass by. I would like to nominate one of my students as one of the candidates. I've asked him to write about "adultery." I think the result is not half bad. What do you think?

Looking forward to seeing you soon.

Mille bisses,

Jacques

"How can we know that he didn't have his boyfriend write it?" said Mr. Oliver.

"Ollie, what does this have to do with anything? And let's not make more of things that've already been left in the past," answered Mrs. Simi. "Maybe he really wants to help in his own way."

"Or, to complicate things!" he said. "Where did this art student come from now?" he babbled. Nevertheless, according to the "agreement," they had to have Jacques' approval to finalize matters. So, they had to evaluate and share their opinions after reading what came along with the note.

Six ～

Thou shall not commit adultery

My name is Ryan. Ryan Whitney. I am an art history student. I was working on a project for my major dealing with symbolism in Medieval Europe – and I am not even going into the fact that I was about to take it a step further to a three-dimensional modelling with the help of the technology we have at hand now, before I was held captive with "adultery'."

"Ryan Whitney" is an alias. I thought using one would be more compelling. I also thought the only way to tackle this business of adultery, which Prof. Arlo put forth as a prerequisite to start working on one of his projects that I am dying to participate in, is to have a broad perspective.

I am gay. This is not something I hide. And the reason I am mentioning it is that I believe his call for a gay guy to write about this subject goes hand-in-hand with his expectation to have adultery discussed in a manner far beyond the sexual taboo it may once have had. I believe he is seeking something far deeper than a simple deception, a double cross of the opposite sex…

perhaps an adaptation of "nothing is what it seems" to express a prohibition.

First, I had to know what I was looking for and get ready: I want to decipher the encryptions of "forbidden love." I want to question why the forbidden is forbidden.

Could this be an ancient written code, a document that once existed only to get destroyed later? Maybe there is another clue suggesting some other scenario than that of the intended relation between two people? Something written far earlier than anything we know of? Or perhaps it was drawn? An intention that lost its original state; that was corrupted, rusted, lost its posture… This is what I need to find.

As I roll a David's Star in my hand, I realize:

On the triangle facing up, there are men, fire, and other realms.

On the triangle facing down, there are women, water, and Earth.

And no matter how many times I roll the star, one triangle always faces up and the other down.

How graciously does this six-pointed star resemble the supremacy of the Creator and the fragility of us humans?

When I think about human fragility, my mind wanders toward that spectacular painting. And I picture it right at the just height so that everything -but everything- can only take place in between that famous scene and my eyes. Then, with eyes half-closed, I imagine that there is an eternal void above and below and I let myself in. Thus, it surrounds me 360 degrees and takes me within.

***

What is this place, this realm? My imagination is crumbled and scattered around that shore. I am by the water, but the sound of gentle splashing does not calm me as it usually does. It is this noxiousness that troubles me, not the uncommon view right in front of me.

My eyes wander around those almost unusual seashells scattered about. It is as if they are fidgeting. Not the nude girl in the bell glass but the one on the altar catches my eye. Holding my breath, I watch the painting come to life. I can smell the dampness in the air now; I liken it to the scent of lemon balm. This strong stillness starts cracking once the hands of the girl on the altar reach where her legs meet. With slight movements, she puts herself in motion. Her nipples harden, a delicate groan escapes her lips. As she moves back and forth rhythmically, one of those formless seashells start to rise. At that moment, I realize that seashell is the stagnant form of a young girl with her head, arms, and legs tucked into a womb. Standing up, she sways next to the altar to kneel. She buries her face in between the now squirming legs of the moaning woman. At the same time, others start to rise and move towards the altar. Young men's muscles almost rush out of their bodies to join with the flesh of the young girls and other young men. Clinging together, they move towards the altar. Reaching the stairs, their groans and moans blend into the mother-nature cry of the girl on the altar. The waves ebb and flow at the shore.

I snap out of the painting.

In the concave world I created out of Hieronymus Bosch's The Garden of Earthly Delights, I am waiting as if in a carousel for a thousand-year old code to reveal itself to me. I imagine a clockwise rotation of people playing their parts like me, all of it happening right in front of my eyes. I cannot call this a passage of time. Time only passes for us; not for occurrences. Each and every occurrence takes shelter exactly where it takes place. And this is why it is I, who needs to discover and unearth that code from its hiding place. So, I spin the carousel back and forth like a DJ scratching a record.

Imagination or not, all these came to pass from this earth.

Before, long before, perhaps long before "before," there were "one man" and "one woman." As time passed by, it became men and women not having enough of other women and men. Tell me, how did we end up with such voracious rules about pairing off? This is what I want to know.

I also want to know this: How is it that a relation that seems as simple as "one woman and one man" cannot overcome such an unfortunate vicious circle? When we do not question the vitality of drinking water or do not attempt to breathe in a gas other than oxygen, why does "the other women'" or "the other man" look so inviting? Why do we reach for the "other?" For centuries, through one civilization after the other, why are we trying to get away with that earliest contract depicting "one woman and one man?" For pleasure?

When go into the back streets of life, I see that humans are not that primitive. Neither a woman only enjoys making love, nor does a man get satisfaction out of the desire to fight. "Pleasure" is the satisfaction the soul enjoys beyond sexuality. So much so that a woman may rise as a hunter drawing strength from the masculinity embedded in her; and a man may be love-crazed once embracing what is in his heart.

I think of the Maid of Orleans in her armor in that famous painting; I salute this eternal hero not afraid and never regretful of the man rising in her.

***

If we ignore the voices she heard, she was just an ordinary peasant. But how can anyone ignore those visions? Perhaps the angels had whispered that famous prophesy in her ears, who knows? "A virgin would expel the enemies and install the unfortunate Prince as the King..."

This virgin warrior would never give up not because of revenge but because she believed in this divine mission. Until the last drop of blood, she never lost hope. She knew she didn't have a lot of time. She would crop her hair, don men's clothes, and armor up. As she rode with her followers in the darkness of the night, the man in her would ascend to life. She would lead the soldiers, who would respect her and not size her up with her female curves in mind. She would suppress her desires, emotions, passion even facing death to revive that hero in her to rewrite history. Her enemies would rape her before burning her at the stake to defy the famous prophecy. Legend has it that she looked like an innocent child while burning in surrender.

Then, the famous tapestries of the Medieval Age pass my eyes.

It could not get any better than that: he was one of the 12 Knights of the Round Table. With all his heroism aside, he madly loved a woman; 'The King's wife. The revelation of their secret affair would saw the seeds of despair among the knights so much that Sir Lancelot would be cast to one corner and Guinevere to another. This commotion, this fear of death, the grief of the forbidden love, would make one go into seclusion and the other into the convent.

I am touched when a Knight cries with his ever-strong arms and legs shattering and tears running dry; when he hides the sorrow of a mourning woman safely behind his monumental body; when he does not forsake that mourning woman. When things are never the same for that epic Knight… This is when I am touched.

***

A Knight who can love with such gentleness that only a woman can possess… I think of those majestic men who are not afraid of that gentleness. Being so, they are just what life is.

If a woman can make peace with the fighter in her and a man can embrace the lover in him; perhaps they both will be more appreciative of each other; more perceptive. And "one woman with one man" will perhaps have a better chance to survive.

But then again, there always exists human fragility.

The history of human weakness is rich with sexuality lived out in groups, sexuality once tasted never to be repeated, and sexuality not at all practiced. One owes it to oneself to reach for the soul who abides within their bodies and make truce with it.

The star in my hand twinkles. "Yes," I say to the triangle facing up. "Pleasure to whatever cost has been our weakest point."

What they have sent down to us from up above has not always been pleasing.

To become derailed, go astray, act inhumanly for the sake of pleasure… Sometimes these were the results.

Biting the apple, opening the box, looking the other way… Why if not for pleasure?

Everyone has the responsibility to guard their elixir of life. Everything is for humans, except the right to waste away the reflection of life safe kept in the umbilical cord. Animals may; it is forgivable. They are not the ones, after all, bestowed with the power to think with that touch of the magical wand. It is us who holds that might. A human shall think, understand, and feel. It is what is expected. At least finally one day…

Otherwise, you see, cities full of people vanish into the shadows…

Those shadows…It is because of those shadows that we go back to square one…time and again.

It is simple actually; very simple: The hidden code I have been seeking says, "Do not let the shadows take over the bodies."

This is what we need to be set apart: 'Shadows and Bodies'.

Sexuality is a single must as it is a precondition of our progression. How we approach it is a reflection of our history. We look for prosperity through it; offer our gratitude by means of it; and use, abuse, scare, give hope, and even kill people for it.

It is sexuality that may take down empires as well as build the new ones. The lust it unleashes, the power it bestows…

That is why we should guard the bodies from the shadows.

Those who can relate to the female in them…

Those who can relate to the male in them…

Guard your bodies; bring harmony to balance.

I used to imagine that people come to life after being cast in their own special molds in the upper worlds. Like Nutcrackers; but with a full-blown soul. Every single one of them was different from the other. For everyone there would be only one partner. The nuance that made each person unique would be the key to completing one another; like that certain bulb lighting only when in that certain socket.

When you meet a man, who understands the woman in him…

When embraced by that woman who calms down the man in her…

One, not a few; only one:

When the triangles get a signal from above…

When the triangles lay a bed here below…

It is then the shadows will not be cast upon the bodies. It is then the fire and water will come together; neither the former will be put off nor the later will evaporate.

It is then you can reach out…And be thankful.

***

What Ryan didn't know when he finally deciphered the codes of adultery and finished his last words was that Archangel Samuel was most possibly watching over him. Not only to support Ryan's creativity, but also to give hope; presaging a union to those souls discouraged to find one another.

In the park view apartment, however, the silence was so strong that it could crack down the walls. Both Mrs. Simi and Mr. Oliver knew what this meant. If they were nominating two, maybe three people, Jacques Arlo had all the right to insist on at least one candidate. But how successful could this student be —who called himself "Ryan Whitney" - even if he were to work with Mr. Aziz?

Nevertheless, it was not over yet. What would Hilda Kenwood say to all these? They both lightened up as if they read each other's mind. Hilda Kenwood would not go after Klara and Jan; she wouldn't have the time for it: She would be busy giving a hard time to Jacques Arlo because of his choice.

"Thank the north winds," said Mr. Oliver to Mrs. Simi. "And let Hilda take care of this."

They could relax a bit now.

"It was actually interesting that he used Hieronymus Bosch," said Mrs. Simi "How do you suppose he thought of it?"

She would have more to go on, but Mr. Oliver sharply looked down at her "Please don't start."

They went into the next room for some tea and sandwiches.

Hilda Kenwood and Jacques Arlo

His bespoke pants were surely the work of a talented tailor, as was the dress shirt. "Obviously he is trying to calm me down wearing a well sewn shirt," Hilda Kenwood thought to herself. They'd met in the tea room of the Brown Hotel. It was a last-minute reservation, but surely nothing that couldn't be arranged for Mrs. Kenwood.

With her classic two-piece suit that would look contemporary in any era, her hair backcombed, her brooch carefully chosen for an afternoon tea; she was sitting in front of Jacques Arlo with a glorious elegance. They were trying to downplay the fact that they were secretly waiting for the young pianist to get started. Until tea was served, they only engaged in a small talk.

Jacques Arlo was playing with his signet, an accessory he'd worn since he was a young man; and he was trying hard not to check the time on the watch tucked into his camel tweed jacket. As the first melodies rose from the piano, so Mrs. Kenwood changed the conversation.

"I don't know what to tell you Jacques," she began her monologue. "Did you really think this art student had a chance? Or did you lose your mind and feel the urge to have fun with us? If you think you are being witty, trust me, I am not having much fun! We do not find much to enjoy on this side of the ocean nowadays, but this was really the last pitiful drop. We have our differences with Rosa. When I was thinking that she would be the one to come up with eccentric choices – let's just say to annoy me - because of this art designer…" and she didn't hesitate to continue as Jacques Arlo corrected the 'designer' with 'student,' "I find it most unfortunate that I will now have to judge her choices more sympathetically."

As did the other three, Hilda Kenwood had also read the chapter "six" and decided to meet with Jacques in London before things got out of hand.

In their youth, they would spend weekends in the summer time in the mansions of mutual friends of their families. This whole bunch was either long distant relatives or extended families. Rosa, Ollie, Hilda, and Jacques had long been living lives intertwined in each other's. And Jacques once again remembered with a vague smile that Hilda was the one who would have the most dramatic first and last sentence in their conversations.

Hilda came from tradition and went on to live the same way. She was married in London and built her family life between the city with a country home for hunting. She was a well sought socialite. Her peerage was undisputable, and her word would be the last when asked of her opinion. Her daunting omniscience and doggedness could alienate people, yet her riches and affluence would inevitably lure them back. This well-planned life in a way was a blessing for her, since she was all already eager to go for it. When it came to Hilda Kenwood's life, everything was harmonized; and she enjoyed it. If there was anything unpleasant and to be corrected about her life, she surely would excel at taking care of that as well.

Tea was already being served. She turned down the white gloved waitress asking if they would like some more scones with the flick of her hand and had a quick look at Jacques. Moving closer to him, she whispered, "What else are we going to witness? Was she not eastern European?" Before the second wave of the 'degeneration of tradition' speech hit him, Jacques took the lead. Even at his age, sparks of wit gleamed in his blue eyes and almost radiated to Piccadilly at this time of day.

"I've missed London," Jacques Arlo said, ignoring her attempt to reclaim dominance in the conversation as Hilda Kenwood intervened by injecting her comment, "you were here just last month." He was a professor in the end, and he wouldn't give into such gimmicks. "But our last tea time was not so successful," he continued. "Same scone, same cream and jam, but unsuccessful." Hilda Kenwood flicked her hand as if to say 'don't remind me' but did not go so far as to comment out loud.

"This past month I kept thinking about this, Hilda. Why the same ingredients failed? Do you know what I concluded at last? Us, you and I, we like to have our teas at the Brown Hotel. Despite the savory we enjoy – the sandwiches, the pastries- in actuality, we take pleasure in listening to the piano here. When we pause; when we want those few minutes to ourselves or just because it suits us, we fall back on the comfort, the relief it provides. Sometimes by mutely following the same rhythm; we sit here to role play what is real and lucid."

Jacques was sincere and loving as he continued. "You know that I mean *I miss you* when I say I missed London. As the years pass by, I have cherished your tolerance and support despite your strict boundaries, you know. Had you not had my back in those fired up years, I would have either fallen off the cliff or jumped down myself. Things were different then. Even today, tolerance is offered in only select parts of the world towards the choices of people like me, let alone those times. Everything was in the closet.

I always thought what you did was in honor of the brother you lost too soon. But, you didn't have to do it. I've leaned on you until I could settle down and build a meaningful life for myself. Notwithstanding your conservatism, you welcomed me with my boyfriend to your home. I can never forget that.

I respect you and your wisdom. I am aware that humanity did not pass the 'gender' test yet and many are still subject to its crucial discrimination all over the world. I do have a candidate for what we intend to do, but Ryan Whitney is not that candidate. I am nominating Ryan for something completely different.

You know that I am not the only male in the family who chose a different orientation. There has always been that group of guys among uncles and cousins, married with children, who would take off for one month 'vacations' with no questions asked. You and I know what those 'vacations' were. And all the women did, too. But that was the way it was. Everyone was happy with their roles in the set-ups.

Had I not moved to America, I would be a member of that vacation club and would never have had the life I did. It was you who made it possible in large part. I have never talked about these things so openly, but it was way overdue. For a long time, there was no need. Now, there is. I needed to refer to the past in order to discuss what I want to talk about now.

I believe that we need an accompanying team who are plugged in, receptive and grounded in art: guardians who draw strength from art, who define success with art, and who lead with art. I nominated Ryan Whitney because of the future he represents. Oh, there are so many Ryans out there… We need to tap their potential and we need to promote them. And I know we have the means to do so.

I think more and more that the balance between drawbacks and advancement in the world today is very much like hot and cold air. When one withdraws, the other infiltrates the space immediately, stealthily. 'Progression' is so relative that when you wish that the underdeveloped is overridden by it, the particulars that you hope to take preeminence may be so different as black and white in different parts of the world. What one calls advancement may be viewed as degeneration by many others. And when one resorts to persuasion by way of debating, one may fall farther back than square one.

I believe the best way to achieve an embracement between advancement and modernity without offending a whole lot of people is to pursue the way of art. At the end of the day, art is the most fair and impartial. Colors on a painting, notes on a sheet, or curves of a sculpture don't lie. As people see and listen, they will want to do it more and more. There are no more than seven notes on a scale. That is why I emphasize music. It is always seven notes to any and all ears.

The world needs, more than ever, 'the art' and we can help give it. We can beat what lacks advancement with art; we can fill the void with it. Not everything will change suddenly, of course. But today we can start from right here."

Jacques Arlo was still speaking passionately; talking in a decisive tone inherent in those who are about to grasp victory as he was changing the course of the conversation into a hopeful melody.

Hilda Kenwood, on the other hand, did not hear much after his reference to those 'seven notes.' She allowed her mind to wander in that secret terrain of hers, not known to anybody else. Her first steps were hesitant. She realized how much she missed a tête-à-tête with herself. Then, she let herself go fully to that place.

Seven ～

Thou shall not steal

"In the depths of the cosmos hidden is 7," my nanny would say. "In 7, people converge with other realms."

"Need we go up or down for it?" I would ask playfully.

She would answer, "Heavens are 7 stairs above and 7 below is hell. So, you decide!"

I have learned from her that 5 is the number of mankind; 6, of humanity, and 7 of the realms. That 7 continents, 7 seas, and 7 wonders are within an arm's length of reach. That days of the week, colors of the rainbow, chakras of the body – as the Hindus call them - are all 7.

That the world is created in 7 steps:

One: that 7 stairs of heaven and hell are torn apart; the light is ours and the dark is the other's.

Two: that 7 seas let loose themselves from the underground waters and start running in their own paths.

Three: that with the waters, soil and the animals on it breathe life.

Four: that sun, moon, and stars start to shine.

Five: that birds fly and fish swim.

Six: that it is our time: You, me, and him.

"He will be there, too," she would say. "Think about it: 7 stairs down to hell, that abyss, that underworld. Somebody will have to take care of those, too. As much as we are alive, so is he!"

That is how she told me about Satan.

"There will be light. Then, it will be dark. Light again. Until, no more. Him. Us. Him. Us. Seven."

Finally, she would tell me about a 'breath.' With damp eyes, I remember one more thing: That 7 is the number of music. And music is a way of 'touching.'

C-D-E-F-G-A-B.

I have no place to hide; my arms are defeated and sluggishly resting on my left and right, I surrender to my childhood memories right here in the tearoom of the Brown Hotel.

***

Those were the years when Rosa was a solitary child. We were young, very young. It was one of those piano lessons again.

That particular time, she would arrive for the class only to see me already seated at the waiting room. I would slip down from my seat swirling my hair and skip outside for a bit with my head up while waiting my turn for the piano lesson for which I was unfashionably early that day. Then, hesitantly, she would sit down on the seat I vacated. She would wait for her lesson with a certain anxiety, and as soon as I walked back in, she would stand up to give me back the seat. When the teacher came to summon her, she would follow this rather older lady — not looking up, but out of the corner of her eye. The teacher always carried a heavy porcelain teacup in her hand, and opened the door with her free hand for her students.

The memory is still very vivid.

"You are peers" the teacher would scold. "You don't need to offer her the seat."

"She was sitting there when I first arrived. That's why I need to give it back."

"You don't need to do such thing," the lady would insist while sipping her tea.

As Rosa would silently try to convince herself that what she was doing was absolutely just, I, on the other hand, would not see or hear any of this. The teacher, who appeared to be at the same age since the beginning of time, would then start the speech that's already been long prepared and now just finely tuned.

"Does one learn to be fair or are we born with it? Well, here is my answer to you: You are born with it. And you carry it along all life-long. If you are at ground zero of innocence, being unfair is torturous. If you stand at the complete opposite side of it, then it is a daily affair. Both are redundant and to meet in midpoint is what is best for humanity.

You stood up and gave your seat. Evidently, you are a very disciplined defendant of righteousness. And your young age proves that you haven't learned it; but were born with it. You stood up without anybody asking. But what if they do ask? How many times would you stand up? Perhaps until you understand that you shouldn't and decline to stand up? How about all the damage that will pile up by then?

Will you ever say "No, I will not stand up? Because, I can see that you will continue to judge righteousness from the others' frame of reference and will be made to stand up very many times. Don't forget, defending righteousness always starts with weighing in for the other one on the scale.

Until you leave the seat enough times, the day will come when you will be mature enough to start questioning for what and whom you are leaving the seat. This will take time, perhaps a long time, but it will happen. But will it be for someone sick and tired or lewd and shameless? I would like you to start thinking about this.

And, there will also be those manipulative ones who will know that you cannot say 'no.' Since you don't care for anything monetary, you will help those who ask for it without a single 'no.' Whether you have much or not, perhaps even just about right, you will give it to those whom in your view need it more. This abuse will drench you, be sure. What will suffocate you will not be the depletion of wealth but deprivation of spirit, confidence and hope for future. As they fade away, so will you lose your balance. Just like those buildings suddenly collapsing because of one brick was misplaced in the middle somewhere without anyone noticing.

So, where to find salvation you ask? You will need to consider the outcome. You will know in time that by not saying 'no' to the shameless, you are in fact cheating on the next, who is in actual need. The very existence of someone who is in need to pay for his child's operation will teach you to say 'no' to the one in debt for gambling. To better yourself, you will need to learn how to say 'no' before you can move on to the next door and then the next, and the next.

In time, you will master this judgment and start to excel in the 'ability to ask.' And you shall ask, endlessly. As you share what you ask for, you shall receive. This is what is called the 'mathematics of righteousness.'

C-D-E-F-G-A-B.

I knew about this conversation she had with Rosa. She had a similar one with me. But I was on the opposite side of the scale.

If you believe that you are born with 'privilege that is your birth-right,' which I trust you do, I am sure you have no clue about the 'seat incident' that I am about to tell you. But, one may be able to do something about this.

I would not ask you to be fair to those who are not even aware about their entitlements; this would be too much. There are those that I ask of this, but you are not one of them.

What I will ask from you is not to claim things that do not belong to you: today, tomorrow, and as long as you live! I ask this because I know you can do it. And by doing this, you will bring harmony to the world. Well, you cannot bring about an eternal balance by yourself; but I will have things to discuss with you and your peers. And talk I shall, and not be daunted.

Let me ask you this: You weren't even aware that Rosa gave you that seat. Had you known, would you have shared it with her? Think about this. Because it would be very easy and natural for you to hold onto that seat to keep it for someone sick and tired.

I would like you to know that the 'scale of righteousness' will not disappoint you once you see 'the right' not as an entitlement but as a plenitude to share. I wish that you will learn to look after the one on the other side. You can do this, others perhaps not, but you definitely can. Besides, it's in your blood.

And once you accomplish this, other doors will open. Other doors with other treasures behind them… Don't forget: you and Rosa both need to be undefeatable. Your dual success will bear the key for a new era in this 'mathematics of righteousness.'

What we take away from each other with greed and disdain for the sake of sloth and vanity simply puts off the flame of our souls. We now know that once that flame is off, there is not much left. Because to start the fire again, we will need to rewrite the history of mankind. Again, and again, and again… This is the stealing we need to put a stop to.

*****

And that was a whole new beginning for me and Rosa. 'The defendants of righteousness'… Even if we were on the opposite side of the scale…There *are* different responsibilities on both sides. We would begin to understand that we weren't that far apart by being far different. Then, we would need to open other doors.

C-D-E-F-G-A-B: I remember 7 as being the number of music.

I am back now. Jacques is sitting right in front of me. Perhaps the only man who is not aware that he is the one who knows me best: better than I know myself. I, who, have protected all my secrets, emotions, insecurities behind the armor of Hilda Kenwood. I breath out my wishes in 7 breaths with the power I draw from the number of all realms known and unknown. So that nothing shall be placed where it doesn't belong; and no one assumes the power to do so, and the music shall never stop.

"You have a point," I say, "I think it is a good idea to put together a team for this."

My nanny used to say, "It's a still thievery if you rip off one's right. So is to shatter their dreams. With those rights and hopes, they have a different test to pass in life. Nothing justifies changing the course of events with such an intrusion."

"Shall the angels sing a beautiful tune into our ears?" she would murmur then. Was it Sandalphon, the name of the angel? "You are the crown of music, should my prayers turn to notes and find you, would you answer me back? This surely is my prayer…" she would say. Oh, weren't those the days?

Sister Abigail ~

As she was walking down the pathway right by the House of Virgin Mary, she thought better to hurry up. She was a little late to get to the town that day. Soon enough, busloads of visitors would arrive to walk around, light candles, and pray. The growing number of visitors in recent years were keeping them quite busy, especially during Easter and of course on August 15.

As agreed, Mustafa the cab driver was waiting for her at the junction. "Sorry, I am late," said Sister Abigail with a slight accent in her Turkish.

"No problem," answered Mr. Mustafa, a long-time cab veteran of Selcuk. "I just dropped off my first customer and was getting ready to take you to town."

Sister Abigail quietly settled down in the backseat. She reminisced the 'first years' as she always did during this short trip. Had Sister Marie Grancey, a blueblood of French descent, not spent her share of family fortune to purchase this land around the 1800s, none of them would be here.

Actually, everything would start with a little book that Katherina Emmerick, a German nun, wrote about the visions she saw. Then a huge break would come as a priest from Izmir planned an excursion to Ephesus after reading her book. The priest and his group of missionaries went to Mount Koressos to explore the surroundings. When they needed a rest break, they were directed to the ruins of a convent by the villagers and they realized that this was the very site described in the book.

The majestic trees surrounding this holy site had been guarding the humble house, its residents, and their secrets nobly. With the early leadership of Sister Grancey, the land had been appropriated and the shrine had come to see the light of day. They had even had visitors of highest importance in Christianity: The Pope had paid a visit, and more than once.

She reflected on what her dominion had come to see during all those years. They had started to resume their duties properly only after the shrine was given back to their foundation after WWII. As a member of the House, she would always feel the presence of Virgin Mary in the sanctuary, while on the pathways around even in those caves about. And this would always give her an absolute peace.

As the legend has it, in the years of first 10 AD, when Christianity was not yet widely acknowledged, the first following families in and around the Mt. Koressos would sustain their lives and preserve their beliefs by hiding in the surrounding caves. And there was another issue: at the time there was an intense influence of Paganism. Hence, it would only be a matter of practice to take the mother of Jesus Christ for Artemis, for example. Many felt this had to be avoided! The responsibility would rest on these hills dressed up with thyme to both protect Christianity from its enemies and to look after Virgin Mary, protecting her from those who would inappropriately idolize her. Perhaps the same hillsides would learn to safeguard secrets just like this. By hiding it next to a rock, underneath a stream of water, and behind the patches of thyme since the time of Mary.

Sister Abigail prolonged her moment of peace by breathing in the scent of thyme from the mountains.

She had come to learn to keep a straight face in her long years here. She was not a cheerful one. Even if so, she would let her joy, sorrow, especially her fears to be known. She would guide people by keeping a distance. Perhaps it was a defense mechanism she perfected, living in these lands of multiple faiths; a generic greeting ritual adapted to welcome some thousands of visitors who could easily be a innocent, a fanatic, an ignorant, or a know-it-all.

Her responsibilities would not end with the progression of this shrine and the performance of duties related to the faith. There were other liabilities she was dependent upon; which she learned to delegate and free herself of much responsibility. There was a promise made by a group of nuns to a group of families of French origin.

These families before immigrating to America from Europe had a harmless request from the nuns. And the nuns had not turned them down. Could it be because of the roles these families had during the purchase of this land? Who knows? But, whatever was behind the curtain of this mystery, The House of the Virgin Mary had carefully weaved it as if it was an untouched cocoon, and they did not let a word slip out. Until, recently…

Technological advances were allowing many things to become transparent, and the little secret of Virgin Mary became the target of some smaller threats. The protective cocoon was dented yet still holding up. There had to be a leak: what mattered now was not who was behind it, but how to preserve the secrets it held.

They were in town at last. The errands she had to run wouldn't be longer than an hour. When she was finally walking back to the cab stand to wait for the car to bring her back up, she saw a little shop run by a young woman selling colorful china vases, handmade terra cotta pots, and hand painted glass souvenirs.

The shop looked like a stand in the street fair with three sides and a roof, but of concrete and not a tent, spreading onto the sidewalk in the front. When she saw the Sister, the young woman offered a folding chair in the shade to rest in that hot weather.

"Please! You can wait over here," she said as she pointed to the chair and the vacant cab stand with a quick hand gesture. "Would like a glass of cold ayran (a traditional Turkish yogurt drink)? I was just having one myself…" She offered a glass to the Sister, who was charmed by a portrait of Virgin Mary hanging on the wall.

The portrait was made by plastering together stones. It was a kind of a mosaic; but the stones were really tiny. What was more interesting than the sizes of the stones were their colors. She couldn't recall if she had yet seen a similar amateur work of art reflecting the dim yet glimmering purity of Virgin Mary's face.

"You use the colors beautifully," she said solemnly to the young woman.

"Thank you," the young woman replied. "I am an art school graduate. It really motivates me to see when my techniques are acknowledged. As you can imagine, it is far from decent to be compensated otherwise in our line of work. But, inspiration, of course, is crucial. And for this portrait, I used a book that I got from you."

"From me?" Sister Abigail said, looking at the young woman more attentively now. She didn't have any clue that she had seen this woman before. She would not come to this part of the town when running errands. The reason why they had made a different arrangement with Mr. Mustafa that day was because she was a little late. "I don't remember giving you a book," she said. "I am not really a kind to give out books like that…" Sister Abigail was curious now.

"When I said you, I meant the Church; the two priests who came by last month."

Sister Abigail was now officially worried. Which 'priests' was this young woman talking about? Were some clergymen unknown to them going around and about Selcuk now? Wondering about which book she was given, Sister Abigail decided to continue the conversation while staying alert, not looking and sounding too alarmed.

The young women returned with a booklet in her hand. She showed a part talking about the unspoken pain reflected on the face of a mother waiting to be reunited with her son, how that fragile face was so reflective of the flawlessness of the depths of her soul. The language was impressive. But it would still need a serious skill to replicate it on a painting.

"You have translated what you saw very well," said Sister Abigail.

"Oh, no. I don't speak Italian. I had help from a friend for the translation," said the young woman.

'My Turkish is still not there after all these years,' thought the Sister. "I meant to say you've reflected it very well in your work." This would be the end of the conversation now that she learned what she needed. She saw that the cab was waiting on the curb. Mr. Mustafa's timing was perfect.

After the exchange of 'thank yous' and 'good byes,' Sister Abigail got settled in the back seat again only to ask a few questions to Mustafa.

"Is it possible that you drove around a group of priests last month?" she asked Mustafa.

"No, but if you wish, I can ask around," he replied.

"If it's not too much to ask," Those would be the only words she would utter until they reach the House. "Who could be those 'priests' wandering around Ephesus and not paying them a visit?" Her thoughts started to darken.

Finally, the word came from Mr. Mustafa. There were only two clergymen. Had they visited the area before? Nobody thought so. But with their long black robes and white collars, they were surely priests. They stayed for two nights and left from the Adnan Menderes Airport.

This is what their story was: The two would go visit the ruins of Ephesus but would not want to enter from the main gate. Instead, they'd leave the cab at the back entrance. Although they had the phone number of the cab driver, they would never call to be picked up. They must have walked back to town rather than driving. This was possible, and many tourists would do the same. The next day, they would go back up again, this time leaving the cab at the main entrance. So, what did they do the first day? Maybe they never visited the ruins and instead they took the long pathway to the House of the Virgin Mary?

Also, there was this: They would also go to visit the Seven Sleepers but would send the driver back and much later call him up to meet at the junction. What would one do for so long at the Seven Sleepers? It was nothing but all mountains, rocks, and the wild out there. Why would they walk about the hills and pathways but not visit the Isabey Mosque or the museum? This was all from a cab driver who was curious because the two would not show interest in the discounted tickets either. The priests would then only hang around the cab stand to eat some cheese toast, drink some tea, and chat with the locals using the few Turkish words they knew.

It was the first time the cab driver had priests as customers; that is why he would remember every detail well. This was a small town, anyway. Daily chatter would attract a lot of listeners. Tea would be ordered and stories upon stories would be told. Mr. Mustafa was confident that not too much was added to what had already been told. This must have been the whole story about the priests, give or take. And yes, to their knowledge they had not visited the Virgin Mary.

"At least not officially," thought Sister Abigail. "I will wait until this afternoon to call New York." She would take the time difference into account and wait until the people were awake in New York. She had some

hours ahead of her, so she took a prayer book and tried
to find peace.

Eight ~

Thou shall not lie

She put the book aside, knowing exactly what was bothering her.

"When you drift away from reality and truth, you are at the hands of a 'lie.' Once those hands are clutched tight, you can never leave."

This was a note written on a little purple piece of paper tucked away in her nightstand. It was she who wrote it, anticipating that there would be days to look at it and remember.

With a deep sigh, she went far back in thought. Back to those years in her youth, when she was not yet Sister Abigail.

***

In The Garden

I was at most eight to ten feet away from the house. Watering the pink and purple flowers, which would blossom with the sundown and then close up again with the sunrise.

"How many are there of these flowers that can so much enjoy the night?" I was thinking.

That strange man appeared all of a sudden on the corner of the street. As if an unseen hand dropped him right there and pushed him forward from behind. He walked toward me. An indescribable fear rose within me; it felt like a scream perhaps. There was so much pressure that a scream would make me feel better, if I could just let it out.

He was dressed in layers. His filthy, greasy hair was flying over his face in the wind. I remember his glasses had dark frames and thick lenses. Although he was so close to me, I could not have described his face. His presence was awfully disturbing, because I could almost swear that his nose and mouth had shifted places. I remember my mouth being immensely dry and that everything was moving in slow motion.

I turned around to face the house and took a few steps. Like three or five...

As I had my back to the street, I could feel his breath on my cheeks, and I was almost suffocated with every breath he took. Tiny drops of sweat were rolling down on my back and I was putting a grand effort to move my legs which were feeling so heavy as if they were moving through cement. Finally, I succeeded in putting one foot a little further than the other but only after sweating ice cold.

I was only three steps away from home now.

Then all of a sudden, my head turned back slightly, involuntarily, so I was looking over my shoulder in almost a mechanical manner. I saw that he did the same as he was passing *by the house now with slower steps. It was as if we were connected by a hidden wire and a parallel mechanism made us face each other with a crosswise motion.*

Two steps.

Now my head was turned over my shoulders, slightly facing back. Who knows if my shoulders were still connected to my body? My body was as stiff as a rock and I became motionless.

My heartbeat almost forced itself out.

I was scared, very scared.

He put his hands in his mouth and wiggled his tongue at me. That's all.

None of those layers of clothing, that shapeless face, those slow motion, meaningless acts scared me; but there was something else. A feeling… A sinking feeling…

Last step.

That feeling that had seized my heart that day had nothing in common with things that were pleasant, beautiful, and right. It was pure malice, harboring everything that was wrong in the world. It was as if 'malice' had adorned a body and found me; and looked into my soul. Then, he disappeared. What he told me meanwhile was: "When you have this feeling, be careful. Something wrong will happen. Stay away. And you will not have the means to stop it; it will surface just like that. When you know it is there, patiently wait for it to go away. Don't try to be a hero. Don't drift away from the truth. Don't try to look like somebody you are not."

***

"At those times when I am by myself and wistfully go back in time, I wonder how I went through those feelings at such a young age," Sister Abigail thought to herself. She remembered a day when she shared some of this with her father. She wasn't a little kid, but she was still very young.

Her father was her best friend. She had lost her mother when she was very little, so her father had brought her up. He would talk to her often and then tell her that she was "an old soul." Also, the Rabbi, who was a very close friend of her father's, he also called her 'an old soul.' Abigail would not be bothered by it. Her father first took her to the Rabbi when she talked about that 'malice of feeling' she experienced. She liked the Rabbi. He taught her philosophy. He explained things clearly, with the help of numbers. She remembered the first time they met.

***

With The Rabbi

"What is your name?" he asked.

I told him my name.

"This is not your real name," he said.

"True," I replied. "It is not. It is the short form."

"Why didn't you tell me real one?" he asked.

I mumbled something.

"Don't do this. Ever." he said. "Don't deny your real name. Once your name is given, every letter whispered in your ears is breathed into your soul. Those letters become a sound. Those sounds become verses. Your name as your verse becomes your essence in the universe. If you play with your name, you play with your essence. It is not only your essence; it is the essence, the core of the universe as well. The universe is built upon sounds and verses; don't forget that. You shall not destroy the foundation. You do not have the right to do so, especially to yourself. Neither do you have the authority!"

I gulped as if I had taken too big a drink to swallow. In fact; I could not swallow. The faint smell of jasmine carried in by the wind had tickled my throat. And I was secretly embarrassed.

That I had changed my name and that my eyes became red after my throat was tickled.

Then, he would explain to me how to stay true to one's self with the number "eight" and say something like the following:

The number 'eight' is a tug of war between the mind and soul to remain partners. Because if one is more dominant than the other and takes over, one drifts away from the 'truth.'

If you left the seven steps behind and found the eighth made up of two round circles, you are fine: you have the key to the heavens.

Almost like approaching eternity…

Almost.

To understand that you cannot reach eternity;
Eternity: that is something else.

To be a perfect circle... And, two times... To go round and round: to become a pendulum with no ending...

(Then, showing it with his hands:)

Eight: To pull a square at both ends to make it a circle: to be the double of the double of the double of opposite pairs.

But, be careful!

It is so hard to not to leave the side of the 'truth.'

Even if for one tiny turn you tell it 'differently,' do or hope what is not 'exactly true,' it is nothing but a 'lie.' So unforgiving.

Lie is what is not 'true.'

To drift away from what is right is the same as getting closer to what is wrong. Where else can you go when you part ways with what is right?

When you yield to a 'lie,' everything, but everything, that belongs to not just to you, or me, but to everyone, decays slowly and fades away.

Whereas this universe which is built upon verses, has some silent agreements. If the roads crumble rotten by the wrongs and lies, how will what to be lived through, be lived through?"

***

It felt like the day when she had been frightened by the stranger on the road. She was afraid of the tricks that 'drifting from the right' could play now that she had understood how a 'wrong word' could move the foundation. Imagine what a lie could do! She was afraid of anything that was not 'right' to sneak into her life and

~ 132 ~

to push her off the right track shamelessly. This, for her, was that pure malice feeling.

She wanted to stay away from that feeling and from 'lies' until the end of time.

But, how about the 'lies' that others tell?

What if she got caught in that quick sand?

It would not end with her choosing the right path. It would take only one person's heart to fall prey to the darkness. Just one person's wrongdoing, could infect everyone like a plague.

"I am in the dark," she would write in her purple dairy.

"I want to wake up. But it is not happening. I try to rise, but I fall into repose. This is not a sweet slumber. It is a poisonous unconsciousness. I am weak; the darkness drains my power. I know I am enslaved by the dark verses. I do not wish to be a sacrifice to a venomous tongue and a vicious heart. But even though I do not know that tongue and heart perhaps, I am sucked up to be finished off by them. Slowly, with jealousy, envy and viciousness...

All those evil looks... Atrocity...Wrong intentions...Lies...

Those self-haters, judging others without questioning themselves and judging - with what? Pitying themselves that other people remember them only with hate, they are the ones who are the core of that awful feeling.

As they fool themselves and lie to themselves, they drag along the rest. And their one word is enough to infest the others. And the others, they contaminate even further with only one touch. This avalanche of a dark cloud then sucks everyone in. This is how that epidemic takes over, that epidemic called 'lies.' Do they not know it?"

***

'The eye,' 'the sensation,' and 'the thought' turn into a wave to come find us.

I know this.

I fought against them before, and I prevailed. I can do it again. But this time the wave is so strong that I am afraid the sun will not shine tomorrow. I have never worried about this before. And now at six o'clock in the morning, there is no sun in sight. I feel the dark in me and around me. What if it never rises?

Then, I draw my strongest sword and stand. "I am true and real." I have never been betrayed by them. Regardless of how I am dragged on the ground, drowned in the water, lost flying in the air, I'll always find my way in the end. Like a magical wand, no matter how much you lean on it, it does not break; it takes you wherever need to be. Once you point it at the liars, the evil-eyed, the low-minded, the malicious-hearted, it clears your way. And if you have no strength to fight further, it becomes a magical knitted jacket for you. Put it on and crouch in a corner and wait for them to pass you by.

Ill-wishing enslaves you to darkness.

Well-wishing is what I fill up my heart with.

With closed eyes, I call for my favorite mother figure: The Virgin Mary appears. As she opens her arms to the heavens, I see her drawing power from the earth like strong roots do. This gives me strength and confidence.

I am Abigail, not Abby, not Gail: Abigail. I wrap myself up in my jacket and take shelter with the Virgin Mary. She will give me peace. She will unite me with 'true and real.' The pessimism, the worry, the envy, the lie; all that is vile thus will fade away and be gone.

***

So, Abigail never said a lie neither to herself, nor to anyone else: not in her youth and not ever after. She shielded herself against lies and wrongs that could be hers or others.' She was united with light. She became a nun. And she never deserted the God in her.

The hour was late. She dialed the phone. "Good morning, Mr. Oliver. I am sorry to call you again and again. But we are facing curious circumstances. Instead of those biology professors, some clergy appeared to be spying in the area now."

"We will address this issue immediately," said Mr. Oliver. "We have come a long way since the last incident. We are more prepared. A little more patience, Sister Abigail..."

"Years ago, I said that I would not lie and that was my only condition. I stayed true to my word, I have not left the 'truth.' I have kept your secret with the strength I derive from the Virgin Mary. But I'm afraid that what we are hiding is now overgrown on the terrains of these mountains."

"We will not burden you any longer. I will call you with the solution very soon," said Mr. Oliver. "I want to express our utmost gratitude for all you have done once again."

This was not something Sister Abigail would ordinarily do; but she did it anyway. She donned her knitted jacket and went outside. Down the lower path, she put a little note on the wishing tree. On the note she asked Archangel Gabriel to guide those who follow the "truth."

***

Mr. Oliver called Jacques Arlo right after hanging up the phone with Sister Abigail. "Hello, Jacques. I just spoke with Sister Abigail. Things are getting hotter over there. Hilda recently talked about your 'trustworthy and expert in the field' candidate. I have looked into it and I must say I am very positive about it. As Rosa is busy with Gregorev and Klara, I will ask your support to go about with this candidate. And we talked about Mr. Aziz; and that's a done deal. If all goes well, we can finalize everything really soon."

"I am ready to help," said Jacques Arlo. "If you are all in favor, we can start preparing Chloe for her part to take over the project with no delay. I really do believe that there could be no one more fitting for this position."

Although Mr. Oliver was a little shy to admit it, he knew he was in agreement with Jacques Arlo on this very point.

Mrs. Sullivan ~

They were a family who would keep to themselves. Both of her parents were well educated, hard-working, and quiet people. She was an only child; she was brought up having everything she needed yet without being spoiled. There was always a peaceful love. This was certain. Growing up, she had favorite things to do with mom and dad separately. And this was a good thing as well. This would mean that they equally had a part in her life from time to time and had piled up memories. Yet, their life seemed to be of the three of them alone.

Perhaps the reason she loved books so much was because she had no siblings. Books were her mind's eye and extended family. When her friends would complain about the swarming number of the cousins and adults around, about everyone's talking at once, that the uncertainty of what rules to follow and which ones to be ignored around the holidays and at vacation times; she would have to resort to only imagine how it would feel to have a bigger family. Then, she would go back to her books again.

They would not get together with many people other than some of her father's distant relatives. She knew that her grandparents had passed away a long time ago.

Other than that, her mother, who did not have many family ties, would avoid any questions regarding her family. At least, she would think so. No, mother must have had avoided the topic. How could it be possible for anyone to have no family?

She was actually amazed that in all those years she spent so little time thinking about this issue. It was perhaps because it was the norm in their house. As if it was only normal to do everything with just them three; that it was a rare thing to have close relatives and the world would not stop if one did not have a family album.

And she would also remember this: In their house there was nothing that belonged to an older house or generation. She would realize this when she visited her friends' homes and her mother would show her irritability by asking if she thought they were underprivileged because they did not have some shabby furniture. Her mother was a calm woman. She wouldn't typically act that way. Thinking back, she was now more aware that the only time her mother would be behave this way was when she raised this topic.

She would never want to make her mother unhappy. Perhaps, she had instinctively known to avoid this subject, so, she would not insist. And there was also this: her mother was such a beautiful and regal lady that rather than making her unhappy, she would always have these important plans in her little world to make life easier for mother. Possibly, it was the same for her dad.

When simply talking to his dear wife, he would act as if he was trying to avoid overwhelming a delicate princess. Her mom was not a delicate woman; on the contrary, she was a strong one. She must have gotten that from her serene and somewhat distant stance.

She knew that her parents had met among some friends. Their far-from-being-pretentious wedding picture hung next to her baby and childhood pictures. She tried once again with no avail to think of another clue. She thought about the graduation ceremonies, other celebrations, summer vacations and holidays… No, she couldn't come up with any memories, pictures or stories with any relatives on any special occasion. Not a gift sent to her, not one phone call that took place, or an initiative from anybody to contact her directly all these years while growing up.

Until today.

Klara hastily moved in her chair not knowing how long she had been staring at the picture handed to her by the man who called himself Mr. Dreyfus. The man had long left.

"What importance does it make how long I've been sitting here anyway?" she thought to calm herself down. She knew the two people sitting outside around the table and smiling in the picture very well. It was her and her mom. The third person was a chubby man dressed in a suit with suspenders and a bow tie. He was smiling as well.

The man who just left reminded her that the day this picture was taken she made a remark about the chubby man who 'must have eaten like an elephant' to which her mom rolled her eyes and pretended that this was never said. She remembered nothing but that, as if the word 'elephant' had wriggled from a blurry past to burst out of the picture in her hand and echoed in her ears to light a flame in her memories. She now concluded that the chance of such a thing happening was greater than that it had not.

She wasn't sure if this discovery was making her happy or sad. There was going to be a price to pay to hold that picture in her hand, it wasn't for nothing.

***

After a few months following her first encounter with Jan, and as they became much friendly and comfortable with each other, she received this curious phone call from a man who claimed that he was speaking on behalf of that renowned editor to whom Klara had sent many pieces before. She thought she suddenly had a big break. The man on the phone, Mr. Dreyfus, asked if she had any new pieces, as this was the reason he was contacting her. Klara said she was working on something, and that she would contact him once the piece was done.

For some reason, this phone call made her feel uneasy, as if the call came from her lonely neighbor Mr. Windel from the apartment facing hers. Mr. Windel would peek through the kitchen windows to watch

Klara write until late hours. Coincidentally when their eyes caught each other's at the building entrance the next night, she couldn't stop but release a nervous laugh that would sound like a screech. But finally, she calmed herself down, thinking that it wasn't such a bad thing to lose sleep over, that she was finally being called up. Then she would forget all about this conversation. Until the phone call was repeated again.

She was discussing with Jan about the essay '8' that she just finished. Their dialogue had really advanced by now and they were fervently bonded after having "discussed everything that is written down on a paper." Slowly, she would scatter some topics in her writings to find out about Jan's point of view on those subjects. Then they would eagerly dive into discussions that would build the foundation to get to know each other, to understand and to bring them closer together. This strong bond had built an invisible triangle between her, Jan, and the writings. It wasn't love, it wasn't lust, it was something else. They were having sex through the words that came out of a pen and mingled in their conversations.

They would talk about other things as well, such as, Mrs. Simi, and Mr. Oliver, whom she met through Mrs. Simi. When Klara found out about the truth behind Mrs. Simi and the publishing house, she was startled. She always thought that dear Mrs. Simi knew Jan Gregorev through connections and managed to get an interview between the two. She never thought Mrs. Simi was the boss.

Jan had mentioned that the company was not just about the publishing house, that they were related with many other important corporations with objectives not known to many. Klara could understand that Jan wasn't giving all the details about the company, and she was fine with it. She also could sense that Jan was aware that he wasn't in command of all the details himself and this was slightly bothering him.

Perhaps this is why she wouldn't tell him about the phone calls from Mr. Dreyfus. If she were to bring up the subject of "coincidences," Jan could tell her that many of them followed one another after he met Klara. He had found out that Mrs. Simi and Mr. Oliver, an old family friend whom he encountered after many years, were acquaintances. Then, when Mrs. Simi recommended Mr. Aziz as a trusted watch repairer for the old wall clock in his office which needed a tune up, he would surprisingly discover that Mr. Aziz and Mr. Oliver were chess mates. It was as if clouds of coincidences were blowing around Klara and Jan while people and incidents around them were being interwoven knot by knot.

Klara finally sent a short story to Mr. Dreyfus and welcomed his invitation to meet face to face. When they met, after exchanging pleasantries, Mr. Dreyfus did not waste time but brought up the fact that another motive for their meeting was an issue regarding an old family matter. He continued by stating that Mrs. Simi was anxious to get to her, yet that they would like to try their chances just as well.

Klara was all ears when she heard the mention of 'an old family matter' and Mrs. Simi. She got so excited that she could barely remember him asking if she had been asked to write about numbers. She tried to keep in mind the other headlines under "France" and "WWII" in addition to "the family matter." At last, Mr. Dreyfus said, "When you are heading off with Mrs. Simi, please consider this conversation for the sake of your great uncle." He left after handing Klara a photograph.

She called not her mother but her father. "I met someone named Mr. Dreyfus today," she said.

"Who did you say?" her father asked with a strangled voice that sounded like something between a whisper and a scream. Following the moments of utter confusion, he tried to clarify the situation. "I do not know what is happening. But please do not mention this to anybody before we talk. I will specially ask you not to call your mom. I will come by tonight and tell you everything you need to know," her father said, before abruptly ending the conversation.

Klara had to contain herself not to call and scream to both her mother and Mrs. Simi, "What is the meaning of all this?" It was as if she just woke up from a dream and knew no one around her. She barely managed to pull back from calling Jan. She would wait until that evening. It was only a couple of hours until she met her father.

When her father came she was halfway through a bottle of Macon Village. She brought a wine glass for him. Mr. Sullivan traded it with a dram for the Scotch he brought along.

After having a sip, Mr. Sullivan began to talk.

"It wasn't easy for your mother to grow apart from her family. But there weren't many options after our marriage. She was from a well-known, old and wealthy family, and she was leading the life they had chosen for her. All she wanted, however, was simple happiness and a journey without any baggage. The person who contacted you was not Mr. Dreyfus. He must be a messenger who is using this name to ignite certain things. This 'Mr. Dreyfus' is your mother's uncle, who she met maybe for the first and last time after we got married many years ago. He is the person in that photo that you've mentioned to me." He paused to have a little sip and to organize the things he wanted to say next.

"I know you have many questions, and that you want to talk about these with your mother. But I wanted to tell you briefly about the things you should know first. Following our dramatic marriage, Mr. Dreyfus's visit you see in that picture was an opportunity to forget about the past. Your mother did not want to go back. Surely, she must have missed the privileges and opportunities of her earlier life, but she had not even once brought them up. It was her choice. And I was both very lucky and unfortunate at the same time, that she made that choice. My love for her had made me so selfish that the fear of losing her would hold me back from insisting that she could always chose her other life.

I believe you are the solitary representative of your generation in the family. Perhaps a few others were born after you… But I suppose Mr. Dreyfus, who never got married and has no children, wanted to reach out after many years to give all of us a second chance following that last sensational get together of the family. 'Others in the family are not aware of this call,' he had said back then about his visit. But I am sure he had to have everyone's okay before he contacted your mother. Your mother did not keep in touch with him and mentioned that this would be 'better for you.'

She wouldn't talk about it much, but she would say that 'there are responsibilities that are handed down from one generation to the next.' She would say that 'in this age, these should no longer happen.' She once said that being detached from her family was your fortune and she had no intentions of changing it."

"Well, in the end I have two significant questions," said Klara. "First of all, why wasn't your marriage blessed by my mother's family? And secondly, what are these family responsibilities that I am fortunate enough not to have to take over?"

"I understand," her father said. "I really don't know the answer to the second question. I wouldn't even recognize Mr. Dreyfus after all these years. But, I can answer your first question. Our marriage was not acceptable because when we decided to marry, we were both already married."

Klara felt as if she forgot all the words she knew. After remaining speechless for a while, she could only say, "Who knows what answer I will have to the second question."

"I always hoped we would never have this conversation," Mr. Sullivan said with a gesture that showed that they were done for the time being. "But, that would be too easy, wouldn't it?" making a bitter allusion to karma.

"I wouldn't want your mother to face these issues again. But I suppose we have to pay a price. Of course, you have a right to know these things. I brought along something for you to read before you talk to her.

You see, you are not the only one in the family who is fond of writing. Sometimes, the words that pour out of your mother's hands are more powerful than the ones that come out of her mouth." Mr. Sullivan went on as he took a pile of paper out of his pocket. "I never thought, when I read these pages many years ago, that I would hand them over for you to read. But I believe this is the best thing for both you and your mother."

Klara was still in a fog long after her father left. She called Jan to clear her head a little. She told him briefly about what was going on. She asked him not to interrupt, but just to listen; mainly because she felt he probably didn't have any answers anyway.

Had she have given him the chance to talk, however, she would have learned about the new opportunity Mrs. Simi had offered Jan and what his answer had been. Feeling a little relieved after venting to Jan, Klara began to read the pages her mother had written.

Nine

Thou shall covet thy neighbor's wife

My Darling,

My mind relentlessly wanders off to a story… The story of Prophet Joseph… It may be because we first met at my company that I feel this way. Otherwise, neither do I liken myself to the lady of the house who is trying to seduce Joseph, nor do I see you as the one who is being forced into adultery. I would hope that I have never been over insistent, ripping the back of your shirt to make you succumb to me. All I know is this: we may have taken down the restriction that 'those who are not husband and wife cannot be together' by the power of youth bestowed upon us. Yet the day we betrayed our respective 'husbands and wives' by violating our wedding vows, 'ego' was the only one enjoying our ecstasy.

I have always been the one to follow the Father-Son-Holy Spirit as long as I can remember.

I believed in the wholeness of the spirit-body-mind and truly and deeply felt for the mother-father-child trinity.

I am not bringing this up out of reverence for the status-quo or based on faith.

These for me were a whole: 'a three-times-three.'

The beginning and the end: It was completion and contentedness.

I could build a heaven on earth once I could internalize '9' the way I define it. A heaven, where the angels dance... A celebration when the dancing feet do not touch the ground… Heaven times heaven strong…

In this definition, was the wholeness of the bodies of a woman and man, that their souls were mates, and that their minds spoke the same language. The stars had to align, and fate had to have its way. Then and only then would they form a unity.

As I was secretly uncovering the mystery of '9,' I would discover:

Man is water…

Woman is earth…

She was prosperity, proliferation. If she weren't the earth, would they still have the young women carry the seeds; the barefoot women to sow them, and the pregnant women to give them water in those early times?

Love, coition, and continuity are a course of nature; and the nature of a woman.

But isn't the soil that welcomes the seeds helpless without the water?

Man is water, flowing along from the mountains, raining down from the skies, and emerging from the earth.

The story of a man and a woman's unity may be the very first and the simplest one. One that turned from sacred to corrupt.

It is sacred, since it stands for the first marriage and corrupt because it wasn't preserved so.

To me, woman is earth and man is water. I believed in their holy unity and matrimony.

So where did the betrayal start and where did it end?

Did it happen where the forbidden and the sinful opposed each other head to head in a challenge?

You see, betrayal is the very next move when things, all of a sudden, do not add up.

And betrayal, if has to start, starts in July.

July is the month of the moon, you know. Not the glow, the heat, the radiance of the sun but the coolness of the moon casts upon that month. Isn't that why the wars, conflicts, and diseases tend to get a head start in July?

That month is hot and unforgiving…

It is July and it is a forbidden liaison…

A breathless advance beneath the shadows…

With wet lips, a desirable woman and a vehement man…

The seductive scent of the skin, breasts covered with lace, shoulders rubbed with rose petals; bodies tightly locked together. Getting lost in the shadows to melt away in the darkness of the night and to surge in forbidden love…

Betrayal is not exchanging a kiss by the shore under the moon. It is making love, one that is halfway between the frigidity of an eel slithering in the darkness of stagnant waters and the fever of a poisonous sting that overtakes the body.

That place was not for a girl of that age, do you remember? That July night, you and I, cheek to cheek? Sometimes one can find herself in a story beyond her time and experience. Something like that must have taken over that night.

Lovers were dancing with castanets. Glasses were being filled up as soon as they were emptied, clinking together to add to the rhythm of the night.

That night was restless, and it was lustful. It wasn't just the music and the drinks, it was as if the stars made their way to earth to be with us. Perhaps there were secrets unknown to us but common to the stars for thousands of years. Irresistible secrets…overwhelming … Such tropics, in between which those two people shall unite. So, may the history of humanity shall continue.

That was the mood in the air.

Or at least, I hoped so.

And the girl asked us, "What is your story?"

"Oh, we are a married couple," I said, most probably with sparks in my eyes reflected from those stars. And smiling deep in your soul and holding your hands close and tight, I continued. "But, to different people."

Right then, the rain started.

I need to multiply 3 and 3 and refigure 9. I need this, deeply.

With the numbers, you can get to know step by step, the Creator, nature, the human, the woman, and the man.

And what is forbidden…

That the first and foremost of sins was when that which was forbidden was compromised. And that all that is forbidden was reproduced from that first and foremost one.

Today, those in the same place may need forgiveness. What I need is only an emotional freedom, a purification.

You know how you get baffled when you cannot sincerely defend your thoughts? I must be right there now. When what you know and what you say does not have common ground, and you realize things are written down on an invisible sheet of paper differently than how you knew them previously. Then that invisible page takes over… Only a sensation, perhaps just a shiver, is already a step ahead of all you know.

Time is passing, and I am thinking. Or, maybe time stands still and I am the one that is flowing from one thought to the other?

I am thinking about a woman and a man belonging to each other.

And that "forbidden" is defined by "the state of belonging."

In that same city and in another July; it is as if I am yet again facing the same events in the motionless "time." Today is July 9 …

I saw a couple married to different people. I knew, but couldn't say…

Not to the woman, not to the man…

"Do not hold those hands," I couldn't say…

"Do not kiss those lips," I couldn't say…

"It does not belong to you," I couldn't say…

They were so whole, so "one" - like us -

I couldn't say…

As I betrayed what is right with my entire self in flames; I could not say "stop" to this love on fire.

I could not reason why our souls, bodies, and hearts were "one," when you belonged to another to woman and I to another man.

When a woman unites with a man, it is sacred and unalterable.

Yet, I could not say a word.

Not because I see myself as the last person to have the right to intervene, but because I lived to realize that what I learned through feelings well precedes what I know as right.

I thought about the worlds where fate was designed by fate makers and impervious. There are worlds like that… When you try to change fate, barriers come forth. When you remove the barriers, the roads change. You simply need to live through it to arrive at "destiny."

But what if you fall in love when it is not "written" in your destiny? What if the fate makers were mistaken?

And I remembered David…and Bathsheba…

David desired Bathsheba so much so that he did unspeakable things to separate her from her husband. When his efforts were of no use, David fell into deeper, hopeless love. One intrigue after the other followed until the husband finally died. David had his Bathsheba, and he also had a price to pay, in the end.

When history wrote the story of David and Bathsheba, it made a final note that "She was David's all along."

So, were the fate makers mistaken? Was that love written when the first chart was drawn? And had that chart been lost?

In David's case, that love was the legitimate love then, right? It was the love that was fated, written in those first charts, a love for which a price was paid to change history.

In the creation stories, whoever is predicted to be your fated partner is who you belong to in the end. If you are connected with your soul, body, mind, and love, and madly so, know this: your story is set from the first chart.

Don't be scared and remember David.

He was told: "She is yours. Bathsheba is yours; and she's been yours from the beginning."

If you know and if you are sure deep down in your soul that this is "it," and if you are ready to give up everything to have it — and never regret your choice.

Then!

Perhaps, then…

***

Klara carefully folded the letter and treated it as a valuable treasure. She was touched by the love and sorrow in the lines. She felt as guilty as if she peeked through a keyhole to pry on a room she had no right to see. All this was even harder to bear because the letter had been written by her mother. She'd just invaded her mother's privacy! The woman who'd always been so beautiful, elegant, regal, and distant… It wouldn't make a difference that she had her father's permission. She was remorseful, as if she'd cracked the crystal…But whether she liked it or not, she had to walk through the door she opened.

She prayed for her mother that night, that she found peace after living a life based not on duty but instead of love, with all her being, with lust yet sadness… That night, she called on Archangel Jeremiel. For guidance to sort all these past memories... And for forgiveness.

The Dreyfus Family ~

Jessie Sullivan woke up that morning with puffed eyes, a heavy heart, and a dry mouth at a loss for words. Her husband had come home late the night before and told her what was going on to prepare her for the day ahead. Klara would probably call early in the morning. But by the looks of the ringing phone, she was calling earlier than expected.

After taking a deep breath, she answered and heard a stranger's voice.

"Mrs. Sullivan, I am sorry to disturb you this early in the morning. But it is about your daughter, Klara. It may be a very important turning point for her. This is why I am bothering you at such an early hour."

Mrs. Sullivan asked, "Is my daughter okay?"

"I am sure she is," the stranger said and quickly added, "I am sorry, Mrs. Sullivan. I haven't introduced myself. This is Rosa Simi. I am Klara's friend and mentor. I'm sure she has mentioned my name."

"Oh, sure," Mrs. Sullivan lied. She didn't really know what was going on in Klara's life lately. As she wondered what the mentoring could be about, she remembered Klara mentioning that she had made some serious progress in her writing.

After pressing a little further, Mrs. Simi became confident that Klara had not gone into any details about her writing. "Did she tell you about the numbers?" she asked;

Klara never mentioned anything about "numbers." But this reference rang a bell in Jessie Sullivan's mind. With no concern about getting caught off guard for her trembling voice, she sighed. "Did you say numbers?"

"Jessie," Mrs. Simi almost whispered. "Please forgive me calling you Jessie just this once. I am also an old friend of your Aunt Olivia. I remember you playing when you were very young. You wouldn't recall, at the big house…"

Something that would never have ordinarily happened, happened. Tears started to roll down Jessie Sullivan's cheeks. All the things she had heard since last night; the essays on numbers that hit like lightning with this phone call from a stranger, and now the memories of her Aunt Olivia and the big house finally knocked the wind from her lungs and she fell to her knees.

After a short silence, she said, "I am sorry. It's been so long since I've seen Aunt Olivia…. Could you tell me, what kind of turning point are you talking about?"

"I can imagine that you haven't seen her," said Mrs. Simi. "We haven't seen each other for a very long time, either. Lately, though, I understand old Dreyfus is trying to stir the waters. Please forgive me that I address your uncle as such. But, we are people of the same path, walking on the opposing sides. To express myself, to avoid scaring Klara and spoiling all the progress she's made so far, I would like to get together with you this afternoon. I am sure Klara will call you this morning. At least I know that she said so to Jan Gregorev last night."

"Jan Gregorev?" Jessie Sullivan asked as she attempted to get more details and only got annoyed with herself, realizing that she really had no clue about what was happening in Klara's life.

Mrs. Simi simply replied, "Kids grow up so fast, don't they?"

Did the life that taught her to isolate herself from others make her so dull that she was this distant from her own daughter? Jessie Sullivan was just realizing that her tedious life was peaceful under layers of numbness.

"There is no going back, is there Mrs. Simi? I mean, Aunt Olivia and all the baggage that has been carried all these years…" She was almost pleading.

"Forgive me, Jessie…" said Mrs. Simi. "It is time to leave behind the past. But by discussing and bringing certain things to light, perhaps adding some details you do not know, I'd like to complete this puzzle. Please take the time to talk to Klara."

Mrs. Sullivan interrupted. "Yes. And then, please join us for tea."

***

The phone rang as soon as she hung up. It was Klara. Her mother invited her over for breakfast before Klara had a chance to timidly ask her if she was available to meet that day.

Klara was nervous, it felt as if she was going to meet a stranger. Should she get some cinnamon buns? Her mother liked those. "Don't be ridiculous!" she said to herself. "You are looking for answers, you are not visiting a stranger."

After about an hour, she found herself at the doorstep of her parent's home. She didn't make much of her mother's changed expression. Jessie, on the other hand, was thinking she was becoming younger while rapidly aging at the same time. That day, she was being relieved of her baggage while freeing the way for Klara to go down a path she might never have imagined was possible – and she could make the decision to forgo it, too – Jessie would make sure that her daughter had that choice.

Jessie, as if randomly, opened the subject, saying "You now know that my forbidden love with your father is the basis of our family's foundation. But today, this is not what I want to talk about."

Klara, amazed that the subject had been opened and then closed so smoothly, became further baffled as she stepped into the room. She almost dropped the pastries in her hand on to the tea table. Every inch of the table was covered with pictures.

"I haven't destroyed all of these, of course," her mother said, holding one in her hand. "Aunt Olivia has a very special place above all. Look, this one sitting in the middle… You can see her in this other picture, right there…" and on she went.

"When I was little, one story she told really captivated me. Aunt Olivia liked this big, old mansion so much that she asked her husband to buy it. She had married very young and her husband, being very much fond of her, tried everything to buy that house. But there was a problem: the mansion was not for sale. Yet Aunt Olivia would constantly talk about how she would renovate it and make it beautiful, and how she wished that the old house would be hers, surely believing that she would bring much life to it. She got especially fixated on the birdbath in the front yard.

Then one day she realized that with her wishes and prayers, she was forcing the owners of the house out of their home. She became sad and embarrassed, and she changed her prayers so that she could buy an old and beautiful mansion that was being sold willingly by its owners.

Not long after, her prayers were answered. The owner of this other mansion really liked Aunt Olivia and her husband very much. In their long conversations, he expressed his intent to leave his land to them. And although he had no knowledge of the previous experience, he left the century-old birdbath in the garden to the special care and safe keeping of Aunt Olivia.

"I learned to make a wish rightfully back then," Aunt Olivia said. "When I say rightfully, I mean a wish that I will not be ashamed of or feel bad about afterwards."

Mrs. Sullivan continued, "My wish was to keep you safe from the past, to give you a weightless future, not to disturb your life. But it looks like that was not possible. I understand this now and I've decided to prepare you as quickly as possible for what may be coming your way. I, too, am changing my wishes today. Now get ready for a fast-paced lesson on the family album. We will fill in the blanks later," she said. She began to prepare two plates with breakfast items, which was also her attempt to give Klara no opportunity to ask questions.

For Klara, all of this was surreal. She had gone to her mother with the anticipation of dealing with the pain that her mother would feel while facing the past. She never expected such a smooth transition. When she initially believed she was going to have to insist on learning the truth about things, it seemed that the same was being expected of her. She was grateful for that, as she tried to remember and put together all the family ties and relations.

Finally, when they took a break after many hours, her mother said, "You know how I met your father and the things that happened afterwards. We were aware that we hurt the people we left behind, but we also paid a hefty price."

And she continued:

"Today, I can talk to you about this. I come from a very wealthy family. They were leaders in pharmaceuticals, and they still have a substantial role. The family members were responsible not only for preserving the existing formulas, but to follow the new protocols in research and development. There would always be family feuds, disagreements, etc. There would also be problems on the ethical side of things. When it comes to health, you may disagree with certain decisions and might not want to be a part of some things being done. This may become so exhausting that you cannot begin to tell how much.

Perhaps I made a mistake, but at least my child would not have to live with this burden. At least, I thought so.

Until now… There is something I once knew too well, but then I forgot about its importance and it is called 'continuity.' I should have realized that even if I wanted to set you free, others wouldn't let you go for the sake of this 'continuity.' Hold on to your questions. What we need to tell you is not half finished." At this point she was hoping that the doorbell would finally ring.

"Does dad also have things to add?" Klara asked.

"No," said Mrs. Sullivan. "Get ready to welcome the surprise guest of the afternoon."

"How much more shocked can I get?" Klara thought as she went inside to freshen up. When she came back, she could have fainted from disbelief when she saw Mrs. Simi already settling in the armchair.

Klara, giving up hope of making sense of the progression of events and the speed of spreading news, was more curious about how Mrs. Simi was on a first name basis with her mother than how she happened to be there. She decided to listen without asking too many questions.

"When I met Klara, I was already familiar with her writing. But I have to say, her being a Dreyfus was also another incentive for me to follow her. As I told Jessie, we are people from the same path, yet we may walk on the opposing sides."

Then she told them about the journey from Europe to America. She mentioned that the organization has other companies in addition to the publishing house. Of course, there were also the charitable foundations. She specifically highlighted that they had many models, inventions, formulas, etc. that they retained.

She tried to explain without raising too many flags that the core objective of her group was to preserve these resources until technology and the general population was ready for these advances.

"If the cables are not strong enough, the electricity that runs through can easily burn them out after a short circuit. Information is not any different. One needs to be well-formed and strong to make use of it. Centuries ago, people were not ready for the existence of computers. But computers, although much more primitive than we have today, still existed. Then again, even if science and people are ready, how can one guarantee that the people in possession of this information will not exploit it? That's the critical question: remember the biochemical wars?

Let me give you a present-day example: 'social network sites' were already a matter-of-fact for some time. Technology was there as well. But we were waiting for the right person to service this phenomenon. I think we did well. Of course, the most important thing is to manage to never be in front of the curtains."

Mrs. Sullivan and Klara were listening to Mrs. Simi with their mouths open.

"Meanwhile, there were progressions in belief systems," continued Mrs. Simi. She said that it was possible for many of these systems to refresh themselves following the "New Age" movement. Topics that previously needed audacity to be talked about could now be openly discussed. This was something they were encouraging. Everything was not just about science and technology. Belief and philosophy could open many doors, as well, but these needed to be employed wisely. Where some could potentially be cunning attempts to lure people into scams, these should not stop fresh and legitimate discussions. So, they were supporting reliable people and groups outside the circle of structured religious organizations, but who aim to enhance personal development. In consequence, science and religion - hand in hand - could help humanity take a leap forward and these were the right times for that. As she was making her case, Mrs. Simi was filled with warmth and peace, knowing how well and meaningfully Mr. Aziz would coordinate all the efforts pertaining to this objective.

Then she suddenly thought she had said too much.

"To turn these plans into action, we need to work with right people," she said. She quickly turned toward Klara. "If you accept, and I hope you do, we wish to have you on board with the new generation who will take the baton. You don't have to give an answer right away, but you can't take long to decide, either. The Dreyfus's are catching up," she said. "I need to explain this, as well."

"For many years, we have had people breaking off. Banking on the information we have, they might make some fortune and leave our fight. Ours is a marathon devoted to the betterment of humanity. Whatever it is worth, monetary gains cannot overshadow it. These gains may be massive, yet they don't contribute anything to the goal. We are very strong financially as a group. We do not need more, and we are aware that more is not always better. We can accomplish anything, but we may become vulnerable when we come across people like that. So, we do not easily forgive those who prioritize their financial and personal benefits before our goals.

As I said, there are certain examples of this. We take precautions and make efforts to avoid recruiting bad seeds, but nothing is guaranteed. Those who join our marathon always come from selected families and are well-equipped and educated. If they are determined to do something out of line, they certainly will be able to get what they want. Separating our ways from Dreyfus's has a similar history. At the time, they hastily tried to cash in on the information they had in hand. Then, from time to time they wanted to jump back onto the wagon. But the rules are rigid. Once we part ways, there is no coming back. I need to say this: that train voyage may be more satisfying than any profit one may gain. That is why I do respect the people who try to rejoin.

I'd like to think that the reason that the Dreyfus family is pursuing you is because of their willingness to have you carry on with the family business. Otherwise, I don't think that they would try to recruit you for espionage concerning the knowledge we hold. David Dreyfus knows what he does, but I don't think he would consent to that at this late hour.

As I said, the basis of the work we do is to preserve the invaluable knowledge and findings at hand and then to share them in the name of human advancement for broadest group of people possible. At this crossroads, you can join the Dreyfus dynasty or become an anonymous superhero with us." The smile on her face gave away the playful intent behind her choice of the words "superhero."

"This whole operation is managed by four main players. Klara, the other three are ready and waiting for your answer. You know Jan already. And I think you will be delighted when you meet the others.

Finally, I hope you realize that I prefer you to be with us rather than standing next to David to oppose us. One day, I'd like to see if you agree with me that your standing with us may not even necessarily mean that you oppose David."

Evidently, Mrs. Simi had wrapped up what she needed to say. Her expression eased. Still, this person was not the Mrs. Simi Klara had previously known.

Years helped her become a master in getting what she wants, so much so that she would neither realize her petite, soft hands had turned into claws, nor would her targets feel the pain of her strike: And Rosa Simi was where she wanted to be at the end of this round.

"In our circle, we ask the young ones to start writing various essays as they approach adulthood. I am sure Jessie was asked to do so as well. Just as I've asked of Klara through Jan Gregorev. These essays are like road maps of emotions and thoughts: They point to where and how the younger generation can be of use to us," she said as she sipped the last of her tea.

"But, this essay I am about to share is a piece of nostalgia. It is an expression of gratitude to Jessie, who prevailed over her emotional turmoil in such short notice and with her usual bravery today. I mentioned that I was friends with Aunt Olivia. Sometimes, even if you are on different tracks, the closeness may remain for people like us: we may well be an outstanding example of two people preserving our precious friendship regardless of all we've lived through. For the sake of that friendship, I brought you an essay that Olivia wrote many years ago."

***

Bonded by those complicated connections, which waited until that morning to resurface, these three women from three generations then sat and read the essay entitled "10" that Aunt Olivia had written many years before.

Each three would then dive into the depths of their minds to think about the timelessness of their conceptions.

Finally, Mrs. Simi said, "I haven't had a chance to taste Olivia's handmade plum cordial for a long time. This is of course a very personal subject, Jessie, but if you decide to visit her one day, you should absolutely taste the liquor. Let me know if she still has it in her!"

Mrs. Simi thought that the reference to the plum cordial was a good excuse for these women, who were made of the same material as she, to go back to their roots. Not quite anything else, but surely the reference made to the cordial brewed every year at the old mansion would ignite old memories, instill warm feelings in Jessie, and do whatever there was needed to do in the name of uniting an old lady with her niece.

All in all, what Mrs. Simi pulled off that day may have been the best of her accomplishments in life by far.

Ten ～

Thou shalt not covet thy neighbor's house, thou shalt not covet thy neighbor's wife, nor his manservant, nor his maidservant, nor his ox, nor his ass, nor anything that is thy neighbor's.

I found myself in a battlefield where self and selfishness clashed. Both were so much a part of the other. The road to selfishness goes through the self itself, at least this is what I believe today.

To tear down selfishness and to be brave, I turn to the Lord. Who else can I ask for help? Oh Lord, please don't abandon me. Help me to dispose of jealousy, pride, disdain, greed, lust, and whatever else I may be harboring that does not belong to selflessness.

I am not sure if I can find the roots of all these feelings and when their seeds might have been sown during my journey; but I know this: I am ready to unload them.

This is such a journey…

An old house that I insisted I had to own with indulgence taught me these things.

An ordeal where you are tested with the gravity of your own belongings, let aside the others that you covet.

This is a journey where you return to yourself.

Ten is where we turn around to be.

It doesn't matter if you recount, count again from one, or start from where you left.

All the numbers you can ever use are found within 10.

Perfection: Where one can count with two hands and conclude, finalize, and be at ease at last.

As I approach that point, "10:" I am clear about two things:

As 'self' matures but rises far above, it starts leaving room for selfishness to take over. Selfishness takes the self as a hostage. It is then that you realize "selfishness" is another name for death and destruction: perhaps a sweeter name, but still, is the same.

As you go on, selfishness becomes more appealing. When the clothes you wear, the food you eat, and the roof above your head are taken for granted, the rest starts feeding selfishness. And as the charm of the fittings claim more weight than their purpose, "self" becomes "selfish." And one gets closer to "destruction."

Just as "selfish" is the other name for "death," "self" is the other word for "eternity."

Those who can curb their selves do not deviate regardless of whether they have plenty of food, clothes, or homes. Perhaps that is why abundance pours in to find them. They live nevertheless as if they have one dish to eat, one dress to wear, and one roof under which to take shelter. That is not to say they do not enjoy life; they do—and generously. They are ready to share all of it; all that food, the houses, and the clothes. They can even leave everything behind and start again. They are the ones who are the masters of themselves. I have met such people: they exist, and it is possible.

Selfish ones, on the other hand, are the cowardly. They live with what they have; they do not give way, do not let go, do not let in the new.

I like eternity: to be able to resume and to be able to prompt the "self."

Immortality is not that a body is alive eternally, but that the soul does not fall a slave to matter, to evil, or to others. Immortality is that the soul rises above and stays there.

This is one.

I don't really want to say it, but it is what it is: Once you face it, the fear diminishes.

Selfishness is the dim corner of evil. Once you move toward it, you surely encounter the devil.

If you are one of those who are not afraid to meet and rather ready for the fight, there is no problem; you were born selfish to start.

If you are one of those who gets hiccups because of fear after the first meeting; know that the face of evil becomes ordinary in time and you get over the hiccups. Your timidity will give way to vulnerability, which will sweetly take you over. That's how the fear wears down.

And that's two.

I make myself a to-do list of "two."

Fear to be not afraid.

Do not be afraid to fear.

FEAR

If you are not afraid; remind yourself:

"I need to fear."

"I need to fear if I reach for those do not belong to me."

Do not try to get to places with things that do not belong to you. Do not reach for them. If there is no sign of that house, that money, or that car in that equation that was specifically prepared for you, do not break the spell.

You, me, us: we are being tried with what we are given.

Not with what the neighbor is given.

Don't assume you will be tried only once, twice, or many more times. You will be: both with others' riches and with your own.

I reminisce about the story of the Florentine girl, selling mushrooms.

It was midday, and the market was thoroughly crowded. The vendors were humming almost joyously. Their loyal customers were picking the best of the goods in an effort to put finishing touches to that day's shopping. Young folks, in an attempt to make some extra money, were riding from here to there, carrying stuff in the back of their bicycles and turning an already disorderly crowded marketplace upside down.

The girl selling the mushrooms had the best, freshest, and the most expensive of the produce. The young man standing in front of her, after checking his tattered wallet, pointed to one of the smaller mushroom containers. He made sure to say that they were for the dinner he was planning for his girlfriend.

"This one please.".

"Sure," said the girl.

She handed him the bag after placing the mushrooms in it. She thought that the young man was careless, and in her mind's eye, she could practically see what was coming: that he would drop the bag while looking around, and then one of those hyped-up bicycle boys would run over the mushrooms and smash them. Naturally, that's exactly what happened. The young man was utterly miserable, as it was obvious he did not have the money to buy another carton of mushrooms. He turned back to look at her, his hands empty again.

After slightly hesitating, the girl said, "It's my fault. I should have warned you that there was a bicycle right behind you."

"Nonsense," said the young man. "I'm too reckless these days. Well, can you please prepare me another bag?" he asked as he unfolded his wallet again.

The girl chose from one of the best ones and arranged the mushrooms with great care.

"What do I owe you?" asked the man.

"You only owe me for the first basket," said the girl. "It was my fault you dropped them. I can't take your money for these."

When she realized that the unfortunate man was about to pay for her own trial, she'd known what to do. More and more, she understood that when she encountered people in a predicament, it was up to her to remedy the situation, not them. Hadn't her journey with questions and answers started like that anyway?

Perhaps the mushroom is not the mushroom, and the girl is not the girl; but the story is always the same story.

DO NOT FEAR

Not when you win.

But when you lose, do not fear…

If you've done everything right — if you believed, if you endured — do not fear.

Oh! What a great deal Italy has taught me. The Vatican, specifically…

We had just left the church after mass and were going to my husband's favorite restaurant, discovered during his trips to Italy.

As the owner seated us at our table, maybe because he knew a thing more about faith or maybe just because, he leaned down and said, "There is somebody I would like you to meet. I was hoping you would come today, because he is sitting at the next table. Prego."

When we were introduced, the Reverend looked solemn and smart in appearance. To deeply appreciate the wine in his glass, he savored the sip he took before finally swallowing. Pleasantries were exchanged. I do not know what was "written" for us to talk to him about that night, but my husband mentioned something about "losing," that I remember.

"A loss is not necessarily always a bad thing. Sometimes, to make room for new gains, one may set things loose or set someone free. We must discard the ties that define one's comfort zone.

If you don't give up; can't give up voluntarily; and if you are a truly lucky one; they do you a favor and make you lose. You may then become desolate. You may even cry. Yet when you solve this mystery and when it is no longer a mystery but becomes a way of life, you sit and wait for it to be over.

Because then you know, once it is over, a better time is coming. If you cannot see the good in the one that comes next, you learn to wait. There is a time for that as well. Like the ingredients for holidays sweets; don't we get them for preparation ahead of time, but then wait to cook and eat them? Just like that…"

I wouldn't have thought that the mere mention of "losing" would take us to such places, being the Olivia I was back then. The Reverend articulated every word carefully, trying to make sure that each one of them crossed the narrow space between our tables and found us.

As he continued, the Reverend added, *"Likewise, to 'earn' is not always a good thing. You earn, you collect, and then you get stuck. You get lazy. You don't think about the future, about others. You linger. You put things off.*

Whereas if you share, the goodness continues to flow. It's basic physics actually: you cannot fill a cup that is already full. First you will have to empty it to make room for more to come. Otherwise, where can the incoming go? It won't; it can't.

'It doesn't need to come,' you may say. Perhaps your cup is already full, and you don't want anything more. Or, perhaps you say, 'This is good enough. Let me be.' But things are not static, you see: There are many that are frozen, wet, stinking, rotting, evaporating, or flooding when we think, not everything is good the way it is. Action is always necessary; perpetual motion keeps the world moving forward. This is the only way for continuity. You need to give, in order to receive.

Those who maintain the balance between losing and earning, who has found the harmony within, are against every kind of overindulgence. They don't covet others' possessions, money, fame, or whatever tangible and intangible holdings they may have.

The most straightforward yet painful method to get there is this:

You need to curb your selfishness, aggravate it, despise it, and reprimand it. Do this so much so that you will not be able to even look at it. Not because you will not have the strength for it; but because you will then start thinking about something else. That is how you will improve yourself. As you get more refined, you will be embarrassed by your past, and the more you recognize this embarrassment, the more you can draw strength from your repentance. Then you will choose to surrender. This is the beginning of the journey.

The rest comes after you see that the food in front of you, the clothes on your back, and the roof over your head is the product of 'selfishness.' Can you say 'no' to them? Watch for the answer to that question…"

That's how that night ended.

Those years are almost over… I realize that I cannot turn away only when I do not turn away.

But the questions are far from over.

Years go by and I continue to ask them.

Let there be new questions. I am still "looking out for that answer."

As the years pass by, I can see much clearer that all the questions on selfishness are deeply intertwined with the people we encounter. We are tested alongside their agony.

The roles that are assigned to them that toss their lives upside down, are not only defined to make them progress along their paths. When they sacrifice themselves, blame themselves, are ashamed in front of their children, we are all being put through a trial. And when they are unaware… when we are unaware…

Oh! But how life tries us just like that!

Will we act greedy? Jealous? Arrogant? Sly? Gluttonous? Covetous? And if we do, what will the innocent actors do with those lives we shatter? Don't say "they too will have trials and they too do touch other innocent lives." Because we are individually responsible for our lives and the abyss we create: just like the bliss we shall find.

All of these may well lead to a heaven…

I know.

If this is I; then, it is *you* as well. And him.

Don't take your trials lightly. Because we have irrefutable reasons to succeed in these tribulations; not just reasonable, but irrefutable.

To make a human life dignified or waste it rests upon us being contended.

Ans being self–content.

Because there is an invaluable treasure there.

Everything and anything is abundantly inside each of us.

There…

Where rests God within.

***

"Aunt Olivia?" said the voice on the line. "This is Jessie. I know it's been too long. But I've convinced myself that I don't need an excuse to say 'hi' and here I am. On the other side of the line…"

It was the following morning. Jessie and Aunt Olivia would make up for all the time that had passed with this surprise phone call from Jessie.

"My dear girl," Aunt Olivia said with the same tone of voice from years back. "Of course, we don't need any excuses. But if you ask me, a little courage always gives a nice push; and this is a good thing. Tell me, how are you? How is little Klara?" Her voice sounded the same, but it wavered a little. Perhaps it was the phone line…

"I feel like I just woke from a long nap," Jessie continued. "Even if it is not full of nightmares, a long nap is a long nap, no? So, an old friend of yours had a hand in this. Rosa Simi came to visit me. And she took me all the way back, Aunt Olivia. Our talk crowded my heart and warmed it up. But the pleasure won over the pain."

"My beautiful friend, Rosa…" Aunt Olivia said. "We would always look out for each other. But this is something else… I will be forever in her debt."

This emotional flare-up from her aunt enflamed Jessie, as well.

"You should know that my daughter Klara is a young businesswoman now. And from what I understand, she has already been caught by Uncle David's radar. But you know what? I'm not afraid. After all these years, I think of all the things I've lost, and I am not afraid. I think we've paid a hefty price. Maybe it's not the right time, but I have to say this: I just learned that Mrs. Simi on one side and Uncle David from the other were fighting to win Klara's loyalty. And all the while, I was hiding under my protective shield. The chase is over; and I think, it's time for 'an eye for an eye' now. Should Klara decide to continue her journey with Mrs. Simi, which it looks like she will, isn't she in a way boarding that famous train—which you and I know very well —on behalf of Dreyfus? Isn't this a big and an honorable gain? Can we not celebrate this huge step she takes where she both shapes her life by honoring both sides?"

"My dear girl, it seems that the water has found its path. And, flawlessly so," said Aunt Olivia. "If the way things turned out does not sooth everyone's heart, I have nothing to say. Leave David to me. I do not want to hear any action plans after today. And you can be sure that I will bring this up with him, believe me! Jessie, we have a few wonderful dahlias left standing in the garden. Won't you come, and enjoy them with me?"

Jessie knew that her aunt was not just idly suggesting she visit: Jesse's favorite flowers had always been the dahlias. By mentioning them, Aunt Olivia was sending her a special message, and she was grateful for that.

Olivia silently said a prayer; one she would repeat going to bed since she was a little girl. She lit a candle. Waiting all the while for the candle to be finally put out, she thanked her guardian angels who heal and transform the past and who she was certain helped her reunite with Jessie. That night, she was sure to sleep better than she had a very long while and in her dreams she would fly off to a sky adorned with lights of golden and purple.

The Club House, Manhattan ᵔ

Klara's life, filled with mixed feelings following the day she spent with her mother and Mrs. Simi, was so different now. Strangely enough, all that she had been told had not affected her as much as she expected. Of course, the facts were new to her, but somehow they made sense; and many things in her life suddenly fit together in a way they hadn't before. In fact, Klara felt as if her DNA was at work, making connections in her brain that helped put her at ease with all of these changes.

She wouldn't take too long to share those emotions with Jan; and to tell Mrs. Simi that her answer is "yes." She didn't know how to do what, but she was genuinely excited about the future. In the days to come she was certain that they would talk for long hours and make plans for her future.

Jan Gregorev was a few steps ahead of her when it was about being in charge of the subject at hand. While Klara spent some time with her mother and then took time to be alone, Mrs. Simi was prepping Jan Gregorev: clarifying that Mr. Aziz was not a mere watch repairer, but that he had a role in the project that they would take over from Sister Abigail. She wouldn't go to more detail, only that they would talk about it at length during the next meeting.

After lunch, they found themselves walking hand in hand towards Carl Schurz Park. The sudden appearance of the East River as you walk up the steps along 86th Street always made them as cheerful as two young kids. Ever since discovering this charming spot together, they would come to the East Side to dine in one of its delightful little restaurants and reward themselves afterwards with a stroll to the Park.

It's been months since they'd met, but it felt like years. Their exchange of essays had warmed what was initially a formal relationship even as their souls grew closer through the journey through the numbers. Unlike Mrs. Simi and Mr. Oliver, Jan and Klara would take a step further in friendship in this philosophical cruise and become lovers with no pressure, spontaneously and as if it had always been like that.

Although they thought of keeping their relationship secret in the beginning, they would soon care less and start living their love nonchalantly.

Klara continued to write, and (as if their love would be left hanging in the air if she didn't) she finished a piece on every number and continued to discuss them with Jan. Lately, the discussions were ending up with something more than a dinner or a drink, though.

Their beautiful afternoon came to a pause with a phone call from Mrs. Simi. There was going to be a meeting the following weekend. Both were invited. Mrs. Simi specifically mentioned that she would like to go with Klara and asked Klara to accompany her. Klara and Jan made sure to say they were looking forward to it.

The invitation was for a club meeting on the east side of the town. Klara could swear she had never taken notice of the building before, although she surely must have passed by a thousand times. The heavy and monumental iron gate was opened by the doorman who instantly came out of the adjoining shed to greet them. Mrs. Simi handed him their invitation. After fixing his top hat, the young attendant excused himself for a quick minute and came back with a small box in his hand.

"Please…" he said, gesturing for them to follow.

"Walk as if you not only own this courtyard but the whole world," said Mrs. Simi. Klara straightened her shoulders immediately. "And don't let this gorgeous garden to intimidate you into a corner. Because the incredible people you will meet inside are far more fabulous than the grandiose marble planters, the sculptures, and the lawn that's looks like a piece of velvet, and the rare flowers you see here."

With the weight at least doubling on her shoulders, Klara felt exhausted even before the evening began. Yet, she was truly curious about wat was waiting inside. Jan would be there, too. Was her dress too simple? But the drop earrings she borrowed from her mother should be making up for it. Then she realized what she was doing and calmed herself: her treasures were always within and had never disappointed her. She asked for forgiveness and pardoned herself for this rambling, and soon they were at the gate to the west wing.

"Have you ever seen a Berlin Key?" asked Mrs. Simi.

"A Berlin Key? No." said Klara, looking with interest at the big cast iron key Mrs. Simi was removing from the box.

"If you do not know how to use the Berlin Key, you can never open the door," said Mrs. Simi. "Let's not say never… But, you have to invest in it to find out. Some buildings typically for residential lease still have them in Berlin."

Then she removed the cap with one pull and she had a key with two blades on both sides. She put the key in to unlock and pushed all the way through. She held to door with the other hand and retrieved the key from the other side to lock the door that she closed. Otherwise, the key would be impossible to pull out. Then she put the cap on and placed the key in its box. As they walked to the hall, she explained what all this meant.

"All this is, of course, just symbolic. Neither would an invitee be unfortunate enough to be left out because he or she cannot unlock the door, nor do we fear an ambush will interrupt our meetings. We only remind ourselves that we can open different doors with an alternative way with what we have; that we need to be conscious about how to use our resources; that how all this makes us closer; and how open we are to gifted, promising people who can carry us to the future although we are all self-sufficient.

Tonight, you are representing the new generation along with Mr. Aziz next to Mr. Oliver; with Jan Gregorev next to Hilda Kenwood and with Sister Chloe next to Jacques Arlo. If you think we put too much effort on the last pairing, you are mistaken: it just happened to be that way. Or perhaps, there was a divine sign in it, who knows?"

They were at the door. They gave the key box to the warden and were admitted.

She first saw Jan. He was outrageously handsome. "He is in his element now…" Klara thought. An elegant party, a glitzy exchange of words, the a-list of guests were all in his league. She felt a stab of jealousy. Then, embarrassed by her checks turning pink, she brushed off that feeling. Mrs. Simi was moving her down the room to the back, while making small introductions along the way where they met Hilda Kenwood.

Mrs. Kenwood was softly whispering into the young man's ear next to her. This scene was a one-to-one proof that extraordinary things could become a reality. That young man was no other than the art student now known as Ryan Whitney. Following that afternoon tea with Jacques Arlo at the Brown Hotel, something that she could not admit easily would happen and that curious tolerance that landed on Hilda Kenwood would become permanent.

She would decide to support Ryan's work and would have him accompany her to various gatherings. She was introducing him to new networks and helping his already unmatched vision to become richer and more colorful. She had high expectations of him, and to be internationally acclaimed nonetheless, and she was not shy to tell him so. To be a protégé of Hilda Kenwood was nothing like being one of Jacques Arlo's, and she was never hesitant to remind him that.

Meanwhile, meeting Klara, Hilda Kenwood asked her some questions. With Klara's answers, her eyes silently seemed to say, "Not there yet, but promising if worked on." When Mrs. Simi and Klara finally moved along, there was no discontent in Hilda Kenwood's expression; and this was really something.

It was none other than Mr. Aziz who left Jan's side to join Klara and Mrs. Simi. He had a way of instilling serenity in people. Klara felt disappointed that they could not extend this exchange more than a few words. She would really like to get to know him more. Then she felt the warmth in her heart following the realization that they were going to have life-long opportunities to chat.

On another corner, they met a high-energy group with an art producer, a curator, and a department head for research and development from Johns Hopkins. As they walked from one side of the room to the other,

Klara felt the power of the Berlin Key. There was surely a different world here; familiar faces from media and undoubtedly others at the top of their game: All these people who may even be likely adversaries outside of this room were all friends and family here.

She could now tell better; the woman they were approaching. And she had a minor shock. There she was, standing in front of Klara, the woman famously associated with the city of Boston, belonging to one of its leading families.

"Shouldn't this building be watched?" she asked Mrs. Simi.

"How do you know it's not? Come now… I will introduce you to Margaret Williams," answered Mrs. Simi.

"Welcome aboard, Klara," said Mrs. Williams. "Please call me Peggy. I was just talking to Chloe. What a delightful young woman. I am so happy to meet her as well. I am the host tonight and I will give the welcome speech. I will then invite our four new and dear members to the back room and come back to join the party. You will get together with those passing the baton to you. I don't need to know what will be discussed there. So, I am happy that we have these few moments with you now."

Klara admired this woman who elegantly described "shouldn't know" as "don't need to." The years must have been generous to Mrs. Williams. She was very fit, but her hands showed her age. This further enhanced the respect she was being shown.

"I hope to have far more opportunities to be together," said Klara, moving aside for Mrs. Williams to pass.

As Klara watched Peggy Williams to take the stage she briefly looked at Chloe and they both softly nodded. Klara realized she knew nothing about her. She had an idea about Mr. Aziz, more or less; Jan was obvious; but who was Chloe?

Eleven

So you also, when you have done everything you were told to do, should say, 'We are unworthy servants; we have only done our duty.'

Luke 17:10

"Welcome. We are gathered here tonight to celebrate our new friends, and to show our gratitude to our flag bearers. This is a night to say welcome and farewell and I would like to start tonight by citing the verse 17:10, Luke.

"So, you also, when you have done everything you were told to do, should say, 'We are unworthy servants; we have only done our duty.'"

Mrs. Simi and Mrs. Kenwood, Mr. Oliver and Mr. Arlo did just that: what they had to do. When at that, they had a life tucked in between magic and reality that one can inexhaustibly talk about, of this I am certain. We cannot begin to fathom the sacrifices they had to make to pursue this path. To do so, what believers they must have been: devotees, perfectionists, and more.

The silent prayers I was whispering for tonight first took me to Luke 17:10 and then further.

To '11.'

Number '11' has always fascinated me somewhat differently.

This is that feeling when you realize that you have just the right key in your pocket to open that extraordinary door that appears right in front of you after you are done climbing up a monumental 10-story staircase.

I think of it as a magical cloak protecting a mystery. You could keep looking at it for years and keep guarding it. Then suddenly; it starts talking to you, starts to show itself, and that cloak begins to share its secrets. And what is incumbent upon us is to do what is required when the time comes for the life-long secrets to surface. Our role is to take part in the ritual of adding meaning to existence.

It is said that our secrets embedded in our memories for once and at first awaken with "11."

It is an awakening of thousands of years. Looking for the self, discovering and making a sense of essence.

There are two possible outcomes in an awakening: You could either be totally unaware, or you could be absolutely certain.

You could wake up unintentionally. Because it is time, because the sun is up, because you are hungry, or just because you do so every morning. Simple. Innocent. As is. Not knowingly.

Or when you realize that you have once again asked all those questions that had already been asked under this rising sun and you are ready to embark on the journey to enlightenment: then you wake up, too.

As you unfold the mystery of numbers, and you have a new way in your life, and when you fall and then rise again and pace the way, and as you look for and find answers to new questions, and when you fear and then rise above, and when you call for the angels when you cannot break the bonds with those fears, when you fulfill your duty with a refreshed will, and whatever that duty may be—sometimes pleasant and sometimes painful—then the moment is right. You wake up.

'11' is perfection.

These four people tonight have well found "11." Awakened, they are passing on the "duty" tonight.

The legacy they are passing on is the same heritage they have inherited.

And that is nothing but "to do our duty."

To get to know our new friends better, we will follow a different and an engaging course. We will welcome them by reciting parts of conversations they had with us, essays they shared. This was not done with their knowledge, but that's the surprise element of the night.

I will start with Klara's:

The little girl was standing in front of the mirror and gazing at her reflection. Tilting her head sideways, "Whose trial was I?" she asked the silhouette.

"For whom am I here?

"Can I walk into the mirror? Only if I could walk and cross to that side and see this side from there. But I would want to return here again. I like it here. I am only interested in the plans made over on that side, that's it. And, of course the secrets, as well. The ones we can attain. A lot of times, the secrets come and go without being unveiled. Wasted. Whereas you put them one on top of the other, you dive into such diverse realms."

The little girl's penetrating the mirror and diving into secrets takes me all the way to that soup lady in Chinatown. I think of the scar on her hand. This was another 'x' sign that I looked at but did not see that day. When she carefully scooped the soup into the cup, wrapped it up and handed it in a bag to me, I would see the 'x' shape on the skin; and would wonder how anyone could burn the top of their hands like that. But I would leave it at that.

It was a warning, however; and the time was 11:11. 11 would become a cross and place itself on top the hand. I understand that sometimes the signs just appear to people to remind them that they are there. "Do not forget to read us," they say. And most probably, prepare us so we do not neglect them in that more significant occurrence in the making.

In the progression of life, when you realize, process, and move beyond the fact that you are someone else's trial, the reality of you being a part of perpetuation comes and finds you. As you pass a series of "tests," you realize that "perpetuation" overlaps on individual lives. You find yourself rubbing your tummy with one hand while touching your nose with the other.

And at those moments you understand, there is "mastership" in "11."

A repetition that owns domination.

A serene certainty and resolution.

Managing the perfection…

To be the "it": *The* painting. *The* meal. *The* symphony.

That repetition of 1 and 1 is so undisputable that perhaps its strength is drawn just from that.

We are not only talking about the one who invented *the* most advanced computer. The one who shines the shoes *best* is "it," too.

To that lady who makes *the* best jam: this number is your number!

What is required to be included in the 11? To ace it; to be the master. That's it. And to know who you are.

And, in order to know who you are, you need to awaken.

To be conscious.

As you fulfill your duty, you really need to give your whole self.

To add to the meaning of existence.

***

The little girl had a smile that touched the hearts. Soft and deep, nonetheless. A smile that is too profound for a little girl.

"Had grandpa ever walked into the other side of the mirror?" she wondered. For her, this was the first time she had experienced such a fantastic thing and she wished somebody close to her, like her grandpa, had gone through the same experience as well. For such a short instance, so short that even time could not measure it, she had heard, seen, felt, and understood so much that it was a wonder her gentle body could have possibly handled it. Yet the heart in that gentle delicate body was so grand and the mind so sagacious that not only would she be able to take it, she would also comprehend her duty and carry it well.

"Because," she would say to herself, "I have no other choice. If 'existence' is meaningless and cannot stand firm, it is no different from nonexistence. We cannot let that happen."

***

"They bestowed everyone a duty in this kingdom," continued Mrs. Williams. "And they sent some to protect. The following is a sharing from dear Jan."

And this time I would relive a memory thanks to a young couple happily strolling on and about the long avenues in the city with their newly born. Reminiscing what? You would ask… My life line, of course. That line dedicated for mediation between life and death. It was different this time than all those years of me intervening between them and death. Life would behold a tiny little baby, and I, two dark blue eyes.

It was chilly and crowded out there. Soon the celebrations would begin, possibly to continue until the early hours of the next day. The next day was the first day of the 11th month. And with the parade, in came the flux of people.

They haven't thought of this: of how they would guard and save their baby from this craze without harm. They grew restless. The weather got colder, and they embraced the baby tighter. To refrain from people bumping shoulders, they found refuge between the two columns of a storefront. They gave in to despair. The joy of the celebrations turned into misery and the music into moaning. The acrobats on long wooden legs, the dancers in dragon costumes and the manikins in disguise all became nothing but a scary movie.

As an inner cry grew strong and high within, they saw a pair of indigo blue eyes looking deep into them. Not the clothes she wore, but her odor was a compelling sign that this was a homeless person. She had sturdy boots and a wool hat covering the ears, they could remember that well. But, nothing else. Except the few words they exchanged. "Go towards the streets in the south; it is not such an Armageddon there," she said.

She was right in front of them with no indication as to where she came from. She climbed the two stairs of a portable ladder she brought along and started to shout: "Watch the baby, watch the baby!" She stretched her arms to protect the young couple and the baby she had at her back; a shield of protection from the crowds worthy of kings.

Then something happened: little baby's hat fell off. The young mother bent down to get the hat, the young father became a shield to safeguard them from the cold. The next minute as they put the hat back on and stood up, the indigo blue eyes were gone. They stared at each other. Was it real or a fantasy? they silently wondered.

The immediate crowd around them had now dissipated and the parade had drifted far away.

They were protected. They understood this well. Also, they knew that this wouldn't always be the case.

They walked quickly toward the streets in the south.

***

. "And some are sent to look after the others," said Mrs. Williams, addressing Mr. Aziz. "This is an anecdote from dear Mr. Aziz."

We are at the funeral home; 10 people praying together. Together with the Imam, 11.

I'm sitting right in front of the Imam.

After he is finished with the prayers, he says "With your permission, I'd like to add a few things."

I lift my eyes up and start to observe him. He is young and not so seasoned, this, I understand. He starts a simple and an unadorned monologue. I like his cordiality.

"God has sent the holy book not only to read after the passing but to learn from as we live. Do not refrain from reading it and have your share of blessings at least once from it," he says.

I feel a smile appearing on my face. A smile that is spread by the amazement and the quaintness I feel at meeting an Imam who can call the Creator 'God' as well as 'Allah'.

Before me stands a man dedicated to duly fulfilling his duty. A man who can broaden the boundaries of addressing the Creator to read the holy book and encouraging the others to do so.

I salute him.

***

"And some were sent to heal," said Mrs. Williams, making her last introduction. "This is from dear Sister Chloe."

It was the 11th day of the 11th month. They took the little boy to see the old woman. He saw that the woman's eyes had no spark, and it made him sad. She was moaning as she turned around in her bed. She told them that she hoped to suffer less during the last days of her life. She was neither a warm person, nor a callous one. Just an ordinary somebody whose illness was a step further than her age. She was fighting with the unsparing.

The room she was in did not have much light. All there was was what came from the small window that opened onto the courtyard in the back. The little boy briefly gazed at the sick woman only after the small talk in the room on everyday matters, followed by the woman's complaints, and the quiet drinking of tea served by the old woman's daughter.

It was as if he just saw her now. He suddenly felt that it was not the last time. He slipped down from his chair motioning to his mother that he wanted to go. He went to hug the old woman quietly. At that very moment, an arrow of light came through that little window and struck the little boy in the neck; gushed through his arms and found and enfolded the old woman. The old woman was hurt. But it wasn't the pain that popped her eyes—it was disbelief. The astonishment tied her tongue she couldn't utter a word. She faintly shrugged her shoulder and let the boy go.

The old woman healed; in a few months she became as healthy as she was before. The doctors were surprised, but not nearly as the neighbors. A lot of words got around. The woman knew; but said nothing to anyone. It was not her time yet; and the little boy was sent to heal her. This could have been done another way; but it wasn't. This was how they would start training the little boy of his duties.

The day came when the old woman's daughter got sick with the same unforgiving disease. The little boy couldn't do anything; and didn't really. Because it was no use. It wasn't up to him to heal whenever; he knew this. He could delay it perhaps; but not prevent it. He learned that well. He figured his role and played it so.

The stories of healers are not scarce. And some demand more imagination than others.

"Healing" is not an easy task. So, I believe it is not up to me to judge whatever the story is.

Yet, I believe in healing.

How I deliver it, is my story.

I, too, know myself and my role and play it so.

***

Peggy Williams silently practiced her closing remarks as she took a sip from her water.

"I wanted to introduce them to you as they were, most habitually. In some initiations, the new members need to strip off their clothing before acceptance. And in some, as this, they are made to pour their hearts out.

As we unveil their hearts, we understand that these are people who take their duties seriously: They are who they are.

That is all.

Tonight, these four beautiful people are awakening to their new roles.

She spotted them in the crowd. "I salute you and I pray that you are responsible for the 'good.' Because the other one is not so easy to tackle.

When taking over new duties, deciphering the signs and carrying the secrets, when you realize that what you get is the opposite angle of a perfectly flowing life, in other words, when the 'bad roles' are assigned to you, God be with you.

This is my only prayer.

Because with Him, everything is easier.

Chloe

When she answered the phone at the newly founded all-boys Franciscan college in San Jose, California, Sister Chloe knew that this was the call she was waiting for as soon as she recognized the voice on the other end of the line. Her voice was brilliant when she greeted Sister Abigail; she attentively listened to the instructions and took notes. She already knew what had to be done step by step; she had been waiting for this call to put things into motion—and here it was. She was taking over the command now.

Years ago, her interest in biology attracted the attention of her instructors and the Sisters who tried to guide her into botany. This wasn't a calculated step with a lot of plans made in the background. Sisters had a more modest agenda. All they wanted was to be deliberate about maintaining their gardens and to get maximum yield from herbs and vegetables. With good tending, they could get really good results in the climate and fertile lands of California.

Yet the divine plans must have been different. Chloe was getting passionately attached to plants as she got to know them better and as she was reading and researching further. Truth be told, she had come a long way in her own right. She was finding natural cures to health problems ranging from nausea to migraines, to joint pains and skin rashes as she was practicing with the herbs and plants that she combined to boil and to cool, to dry and add after. She was following articles on the subject and even getting ready to start up her own blog. She was visiting the Bartram Gardens in Philadelphia just for this reason when she met Jacques Arlo, who was there under completely different circumstances. What a great coincidence that was!

Prof. Arlo was very impressed with Sister Chloe after their first encounter in the middle of the plants and after a nice, long conversation about them with her. He would then follow suit to properly get in touch with her after having Mr. Oliver's approval. With an arrangement made by one of her earlier headmasters, they would meet yet again in another botanical garden, where Prof. Arlo would open up the subject.

The matter was about a set of responsibilities that a group of Sisters would hand over from across the pond. They were not different from a family bonded with tradition and secrecy handed over from one generation to the next. Sworn to secrecy many years ago, they were keeping numerous healing herbs undisclosed on the plains of Ephesus near the House of the Virgin Mary.

Word of mouth was that a group of volunteers from Southern France had helped them resurrect the Shrine of the Virgin Mary, and in turn—supposedly—asked them to safeguard these herbs collected from the Alps and some other mountains and keep them under the utmost scrutiny in the best way, which was to plant them right in front of everyone's eyes. This legend also included a hand-written book that recorded all these plants and herbs. Yet, it was Sister Abigail who knew more of the details.

Chloe would talk with and receive some information from her headmaster before meeting Mr. Arlo and express her enthusiasm to accept such a responsibility. Then, she would meet with Jacques Arlo to learn some more. One would of course never know how exactly Arlo found that headmaster and what he had told her. Certain things were best left unanswered.

The responsibility that was being offered was an honorable one. Sister Chloe was already very curious and excited about the famous book and its contents without ever seeing it. Once again, as the legend goes, the Sisters who have safeguarded the plants and herbs in this book and handed them to the generations to come could say one thing: These herbs were natural medicine that could heal anything and everything. And, they had to surface at the right time in order for them to be processed by the right people for the good of the masses.

Sister Chloe would be responsible for the safekeeping of these plants in America. Since this adventure was initiated there, she would go visit the Bertram Gardens and find some precious information in the books in its library. Just as the Bertram was the oldest botanical garden and open-air museum in America; it was possible to build more as such. She was depending on a coalition among Sisters for that; they could safeguard these plants just like it had been done for centuries: in the open air. She had already contacted many convents with suitable climate and started to group the plants to have them maintained in their gardens. In short, she had already embraced her responsibilities and started work on them as well.

***

It was late night at the Club House.

They were eight. According to the rules, they had to have the agreement of the original four who were handing over their duties to the newcomers. Had any one of them opposed, the agreement would be nullified; and they would have to come up with a new candidate. They each had to evaluate the others' suggestions. Had they not agreed, they at least had to compromise. After laying down all the cards on the table, it seemed like both those who were leaving and those who were taking over looked content. An agreement was in place.

Hilda Kenwood, who had not spoken much up to that point, flicked her hand to have a moment after she fixed her angel wings brooch, a finishing touch on her outfit, impeccable as usual. She was prepared to ask the most fatal question of the night when everyone was least expecting it.

"You listened to Chloe's story. Now, we all have a better understanding of why we are here. Let's say we have inherited a book from the past and this book contains rare herbs that are used in medicinal healing. What do you suppose tonight is the start of?"

The question was clear. After putting two and two together with her story in her mind, Chloe began to speak.

"There is always an understanding that there is a cure for cancer and other incurable and epidemic diseases, yet these cures are not made public because of certain motivations benefiting to big pharma or the deep state. I believe we have a solution in our hands to put an end to this."

Klara was on board as well. She picked up where Chloe left. "And these motivations are not without reason. For example, the devastating deprivation of natural resources worldwide by the head-spinning speed of population growth: the scarcity of water, food, and energy… And consequently, the wars… Oil wars, water wars… Aren't they all about taking over or holding onto ever-diminishing resources?"

"This is also open to discussion in its own context," said Jan Gregorev, bringing on a new perspective. "In both cases, both for the sake of sharing the diminishing resources or taking them over, the world population takes a hit. Doesn't this then, suit the interest of the 'bad guy' behind the curtains? Why should he heal the ill and share these resources when these resources are already scarce? These and similar allegations are almost making their way to be head topics in debate clubs in schools, let alone being a 'top-secret topic.' Come to think of it, when you search the internet about 'drugs and conspiracy theories,' you probably get millions of hits. If a topic is opened to discussion millions of times, can it be a conspiracy?" He shrugged and continued.

"And don't forget that the people who could possibly take a stand in such a conspiracy and prevent launching of these drugs come in such a wide spectrum, it would not be easy at all to keep them together under this damned umbrella. Do you think that the researchers at the universities, the food administrators, the grassroots movements, and government administration, control, and surveillance could all come together to agree? They themselves, their families and loved ones, will fall victim to these diseases and they will lose people, as well, but they will not say a word about a cure because of hush money or an ideology? Only a few trivial voices?"

Mr. Aziz couldn't help to jump in. "Do you mean to say that the conspiracy theories about the cures found but not shared are conspiracies within themselves? I've never looked at it that way…But, why?"

As if he knew the answer very well, Jan Gregorev continued with great self-confidence. "Because it is more attractive to say, 'we know but won't share' than 'we don't know.' Maybe to feed a bit of hope to people even if it doesn't completely satisfy their hunger, or just to maintain some level of self-respect. Meanwhile, the labs go on advancing their research easily and without disruption. And maybe this way, they can more conveniently steal some clues about their competitors' progress. No one would really know who has advanced more or who's a step behind. Or for some other, perhaps relevant, but invaluable reason, what is in the market today is the conspiracy theories, and theories of conspiracy theories on the drugs, but the drugs themselves!"

Chloe, who thought the strategy interactively built by Jan Gregorev and Mr. Aziz wasn't too bad, joined to elaborate.

"They know what they are looking for, but they don't know where to look for it. And perhaps, when they do find it, they will share it at too high of a price."

Then they all stopped and stared puzzled at Jacques Arlo, who was laying down Asterix comic books on the table.

Mr. Oliver stood up and took the lead. "I understand that in your heart you are hoping that the cure, which the big pharma does not or could not come up with, is in that book. And I am sure you feel very close to having the answer to many predicaments, and this is maybe making you almost secretly thrilled. Yet, our method serves a far different cause than this.

Think for a moment that the details of the harvest time and method and the harvester of these plants, which we are trying to move to our backyard, are as important as how to boil and how to disintegrate them. There are some that need to be picked by women who have never given birth. Then, there are those that need to be cut and dried by someone with a desperate illness in the family. And those that need to be picked by kids with exceptional abilities. We need to take into account where we will find the people with these exact capacities; and remember that we will need to trust them and confide our secret to a certain extent. Everyone will know their own parts, but few will have a command over the master plan. This is simply because it is better and safer for the sake of the plan and the people involved."

The new foursome was listening to Mr. Oliver with awe nonetheless, and contemplating whether to take him seriously or not. It wasn't common for Mr. Oliver to take matters lightly. So, if what he was saying was not gibberish, where would it lead?

"Then there is the ritual, of course…" continued Mr. Oliver, almost with a gloomy solemnity. "All these things will need to be done between the new and the full moon. We will not make this pot…, this *medicine* all by ourselves, after all," he paused. He gazed at Jacques Arlo, looking for a little support. Did he say too much too soon? He wasn't expecting the thing he said to make sense now. All he was hoping was that they understood this was not going to be as simple as pulling tomatoes off a plant.

"We are talking about cosmic energies," said Jacques Arlo, with a poise typically inherent in a teacher. "All our past memories are now buried in our subconscious, waiting on standby in a mass of energy. All the intelligence for humanity to take a leap forward are embedded in there. We can revive our subconscious and tap this cognition pool to remember what we already know. The powers that are ready to support our actions will also come on board.

Some call this cosmic energy, some call them angels. With some help, it is possible to decipher the codes of intelligence, which is already there and which we already subconsciously know, and which will carry us to enlightenment.

This is not a spur of the moment discovery. Trust me, this is the handing over of the knowledge of thousands of years. A ritual nourished and seasoned by meditations and revelations: A ritual promising to reach unmatched realms by entrusting the secrets to devoted sages, the secrets for which some mysterious masters and groups dedicated to esoterism shielded protection, suffered cruelty, were destroyed, and went into extinction. We have seen before what magnificent ends the invaluable knowledge preserved since the time of ancient Egypt and Sumer can yield once we become one with the universe. Now is the time for reawakening."

"Yes" said Mrs. Simi. "We *are* talking about the elixir of life. 'Eternity' is not reaching immortality. Eternity is freedom from captivity. Not to be enslaved by a human, by a substance, but most importantly by ignorance. Thus, it means reaching for the God in you, trusting the power of solidarity, righteousness, the truth. Not to succumb to lies, thievery, selfishness. Not to be afraid to love and do good. That's when one reaches eternity. And becomes 'One.' If you are asking if there is an elixir for that, the answer is 'yes, there is.' We know that at least from the time of Moses up to now, some great men found the power to advance the humanity in them as such.

And then one day, a dose much less than the usual amount was given to a promising corporal, who turned out to become a despot turning this world into a hell for millions of people. At that point, the power of this immensely powerful and equally secretive elixir preserved at unspoken expenses was questioned in a completely different context. Obviously, this potion could create a beast from one who had even the slightest of flaw in his soul. No wrong choice like that had ever been made up before. It was decided with great shame and remorse that this potion, which could bring out the best of spiritual and bodily power in men, to have not just humans but humanity progress marginally, had to be eliminated. As the medicinal herbs— components of the potion—were relocated for safekeeping, the only hope was that this secret could be preserved for thousands of years and be resuscitated when the time is right.

Did we not see when year 2012 was over; marked as 'the end' by the Mayan calendar; that every 'end' is a 'beginning?' Every end is a new beginning. We know that this new era is an incomparable opportunity for enlightenment. The stars are lining up so that we have nothing but hope.

With the upcoming astral breaks and the awakening mind, it is an ideal time to revive the elixir of life, which we believe we will heavily need in the new millennium. This is why you are here."

Trying to figure out if what they heard is real, Jan, Klara, Chloe, and Mr. Aziz were completely still at their chairs, looking at each other. The grave looks filled with expectations on the faces of others only confirmed the gravity of the discussion. If they were to succeed, humanity would take such a leap forward that incurable diseases, scarcity, poverty, and enslavement would only be history. As the balance between humanity and nature finds its equilibrium, much would be settled of its own accord, allowing mankind to go into a new phase of thinking. Every day starting with awareness would be a harbinger of a better future for all humanity.

Jacques Arlo reached for the comic books to lighten up the mood. "'Asterix in Spain,' 'Asterix and the Soothsayer,' 'Asterix and Caesar's Gift.'" He was randomly arranging them on the table while smiling playfully. "Not everyone was totally discrete about saving the secrets from extinction. There were those who kept them overtly alive to jog our memories," he said. "I am referring to this series, still around today after being launched in 1960's France, when a new set of cards were being dealt subsequent to World War II. Followed by a worldwide audience with great enthusiasm, these two buddies in the series did not only become heroes thanks to that powerful elixir, they also kept the potion alive. They kept those who were aware in tune and groomed those who didn't. Just like us preparing you for tonight.

We chose you for this obligation knowingly and after careful consideration. We undoubtedly trust you that you will understand and adapt promptly to roll the dice. It is now your turn to be the heroes."

Everyone was smiling now. The heavy mood was scattered and made room for a magical optimism.

Soon enough, "Give thanks to Archangel Raphael," Jan whispered to Klara. There was no irony in his voice; he must have known by now that Raphael is the angel called upon for healing, and he was praying just for that.

Mr. Aziz decided to mention that book that the Bektashi Order turns to as a reference to Chloe, who, he believed would also enjoy reading it.

They would need to take off on this unparalleled journey soon, and embrace it wholeheartedly, too. It sure looked like the children of light were ready for duty.

Twelve ᷇

The night is nearly over; the day is almost here. So let us put aside the deeds of darkness and put on the armor of light.

Romans 13:12

I am calling on Archangel Michael, just to say, 'Thank you,' that's all.

Not to mention also because he didn't leave me alone up to now; with my flaws and amendments, my regrets and attainments, my gratifications, my preoccupations, my extravagance, then my regrets again and the rewards I nurtured within. I was always "One." Yet I haven't come this far just "this once" with "one word," "one action," "one injustice," "one victory," "one instinct," "one toleration" or "one living day." This is what I am thankful for: this journey.

Wasn't that *the* day when this journey fell on the 12th day of the 12th month of the 12th year?

There's been times when I was afraid of being bereaved of "words," thankfully they always came back and found me.

We are at those hours when the night is over; and the dawn is near.

Just then, when we put on the armor of light, words are with me in strings of line.

Now, as the sun rises behind the mountain with all its might, I am living in the moment. I know they are busy, very busy.

But later on, when the day gets going, I will have a reunion with the Angels.

I will think about what I have and what I will have. I will imagine the days when everything will be more beautiful, healthier, brighter, and radiant. I will make a wish as if sowing a seed for a clear road ahead, abundant good health and a clear conscience.

I will think of people I know one by one. As I recall every single one of them, a spark will adorn my tree of hope, just like the Christmas tree. Then on top, I will place a star for those I do not know. One of those with a lot of corners, so, everybody can gather underneath.

I will forgive those who hurt me, and I will turn my heart to the beautiful hearts of those so that no evil can find shelter within me.

And I will give thanks.

Today:

On the 12th day of the 12th month of 2012.

I am waiting for the time to show 12:12.

Will I pray more or be more grateful? No.

But I know more people will pray and give thanks at this time. I suppose that's what I am waiting for.

"12."

This is the number where you go beyond fulfilling your duty and shine your star.

And today at this hour, everyone wants to glow and shine. What a great fortune for those who love the light!

What is 12 if not the number of the Festival of Lights?

On the 12 gates of Jerusalem, inscribed are the names of 12 tribes.

They set off to the 4 corners of the world to look after the earth, fire, water, and air.

And they were there for 12 months…

The 12 Apostles of Jesus and the 12 Apostles of Mithras.

The 12 Imams of Alevis.

The 12 Knights of King Arthur.

The 12 Steppers of Dalai Lama.

And what about the 12 deities considered to be residing in Mount Olympus connected to 12 signs by Plato?

They reigned over the waters and land, art and war, wisdom and love and many more from Anatolia to Ancient Greece to Ancient Rome and put their stamps on every walk of life.

Haven't they dominated everything from the secret passions of earth, to the hopes of skies; the battles of smothered passions, sometimes the fruits of a forbidden bash, sometimes to wrath of a pure love, the perfection of art, plants, animals; until men conquered what was so unattainable before.

The wise men, the scholars and those who lived and gave life to astrology, mathematics, music, art, religion, philosophy; those who were more civilized, more advanced, more progressed than us, enthroned the number "12.'

I stripped down all the "words" from the wall.

Not with atrocity, greed, or grudge.

I took them all down so they all become a cornerstone, and I erected my temple.

The "4" in "12" rejuvenates and repeats three times.

Like "4 seasons."

Like "4 elements."

Like "4 living things:" one with fins, one with wings, one with four legs, and then mankind.

In water, in air, on earth with fire

Those who swim, fly, run, and walk.

The story of "12" is living together in all seasons.

One, which heavily rewinds.

If not: a big flood.

If not: a big earthquake.

If not: a big fire.

Rewind.

Until we understand "12."

Since the time of Adam.

Almost everything but Adam varies from one tongue to the other.

As if the diagram of humanity was drawn and concealed in him with "12."

12 hours of day.

12 hours of night.

Embroidered like lace in our consciousness and in our genes.

It is the brightest, purest of numbers flowing off into eternity.

If you can prevent something, anything becoming a part of infinity, that thing does not exist in the first place. Anything that cannot be a part of endlessness is incomplete from the beginning. Even the water you drink is a part of this totality. This is not getting lost in endlessness, it is being infinitely present in it.

Don't argue, don't disagree with 12, follow its path.

I don't mean to say behind it: walk *with* it to eternity.

This is that number!

It is as if I woke up from a long sleep.

Which part of it was a dream, and which part a reality?

All I wish is that my prayers come true.

And, so must it be.

Klara ~

(The Following Year)

After tending to their duties in this incredible journey, the undertakings they took did not give them much time. Klara, Mr. Gregorev, Mr. Aziz, and Sister Chloe would continue to embark on new adventures, on their separate paths and sometimes with crossing ones.

Not too long after, Klara would find herself on her way to Florence.

When finally meeting the extraordinary Dr. Giovanni Mancino, Klara asked him to interpret a dream instead of posing some questions about a scientific theory which falls into his expertise.

"The woman with the mask who showed herself to you was not alone," the professor said, after re-playing the dream in his mind. "You should look for her and find her. Obviously, she will not come up to you and say 'yes, that's me!' There will be signs to follow, puzzles to solve. Perhaps a child? Because a woman like this might only show her face to you if a child is in question. Does this mean anything to you?"

What she was told was surely a precious clue to follow, considering her responsibilities at the Foundation, which included discovering young and talented children. But was it possible to achieve her goals by following a dream, like Dr. Mancino suggested?

Lest it be forgotten that there would be a Mrs. Oppenheimer factor to overcome. The scope of this highly incompatible duo's responsibilities would overlap during this project at the Foundation. And Klara would need to explain to Mrs. O. that she'd follow a woman in her dreams to find a young talent she had been looking for. For Mrs. O., the dreams were fantasies. The angels belonged to children's books. And science was science. It was ridiculous, meaningless, and a waste of time to start off with a dream and follow Angels to get somewhere. This was just wasting the Foundation's resources, and as long as she was there, this would not be possible.

Klara, however, had the winds behind her already. Not too long ago, she was at one of those schools with vast green grounds in Massachusetts. She would introduce herself and explain to the children that, as an instructor, she was there to help them enhance their writing abilities. She expressed her willingness to get to know them as well. Many hands would rise without hesitation and Klara would pick an enthusiastic one whose dancing fingers called out to her. Invariably there was a student whose lively eyes were pierced with a different light to attract the teacher's attention, perhaps with no intention to do so.

When their eyes met, Klara felt that the stars must have just winked at her. She immediately thought with great excitement that to have this kind of a light; "he must have placed all those stars in one hand and swallowed them all at once."

It is possible that she did not know what she was looking for until that moment. But she was almost sure that he was standing right in front of her now. As she found the one she didn't know, she understood what she was looking for.

As she was trying to control her heart beat with her brain, she also had to send a message to the latter to "slow down" as it started the probability calculations such as "Can I be this lucky? Could this be the one? If he is, how will things be?" Then, as her heart, her brain, and herself calmed down, she would turn her attention to the little hands reminding herself that neither was this the first child, nor was it the first classroom. Wasn't she was looking for the "one" in another camp at another campus just last month? This story would start someplace. Why not here?

With this realization, she would get excited for one last time.

When asked of his name, "Errol," he with the little hands would answer. "It's with two 'r's. It means noble, man of his word."

And, an endless hope would conquer Klara.

Now a new journey was about to begin.

www.ingramcontent.com/pod-product-compliance
Lightning Source LLC
Chambersburg PA
CBHW022140050726
47590CB00002B/514